The Cullen Collection

Reader's Guide

By

Michael Phillips

Published by
Sunrise Books and Wise Path Books

THE CULLEN COLLECTION READER'S GUIDE
2018 by Sunrise Books and Wise Path Books

ISBN 978-1791832681

Contents

The Cullen Collection of the Fiction of George MacDonald

THE WORLD OF GEORGE MACDONALD'S WRITINGS

Some suggested reading ideas

by
Michael Phillips

I am often asked, "Which George MacDonald book should I start with?" or, "In what order should I read MacDonald's novels?" Just within the past week I have replied to three very different queries:

> *"I don't read fiction, but would like to read some of MacDonald's novels—where should a complete fiction and MacDonald novice start?"*
> *"What book would you recommend for a woman who has read nothing of MacDonald's?"*
> *"I want to give a MacDonald novel to my husband—what would you suggest for a man with strong masculine themes?"*

Any answer is necessarily subjective. Most would respond according to his or her preferences and tastes. The purposes of a potential reader are also important—what is the best book for a particular reader at such-and-such a time, and perhaps for a specific need?

My recommendations were different in all three cases.

MacDonald enthusiasts often introduce others to MacDonald's writings in the same order in which they happen to have discovered his books.

One of my dear friends came to love MacDonald through *The Princess and the Goblin,* and thus that preeminent of MacDonald's fantasies is always near the top of his particular recommended list.

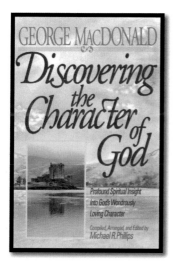

And while sometimes helpful, one's own reading history can at times also be a poor rationale for recommendation because it focuses on someone *else's* experience not necessarily on the needs, reading tastes, and objectives of the potential reader. For example, because C.S. Lewis discovered MacDonald through *Phantastes,* many have encouraged others to walk through that same literary door. In my opinion, however, *Phantastes* represents the worst possible introduction to the message of George MacDonald. For thousands over the years, this unfortunate advice has proved a great stumbling block to a true understanding of the overarching spiritually thematic unity of MacDonald's writings.

Many have also been introduced to MacDonald's world through one of his sermons or through my own edited editions of his novels, as well as the two topical compilations *Discovering the Character of God* and *Knowing the Heart of God*, both of which provide an overview to MacDonald's spiritual perspectives. One coming to MacDonald for the first time could not do better than these two books for an overview of his thought, along with some of the novels I will introduce in a moment.

In my own case, I had the good fortune to be introduced to a diverse diet of MacDonald's books from the outset because no titles were specifically mentioned as better than any others. My wife Judy and I simply read all the titles our local library had on hand. They included both "Princess and Curdie" books, *At the Back of the North Wind*, Elizabeth Yates's edition of *Sir Gibbie*, and yes, also *Phantastes*. I no longer even remember the order in which we read them.

Rather than attempt to steer others to follow my own path, I usually try to tailor reading suggestions according to an individual's interests and tastes, keeping in mind at the same time the importance of gaining through one's reading an accurate and balanced perspective of George MacDonald's overall style and message. Thus, though one's interest may indeed be "adult fantasy," I would still not recommend *Phantastes* as an entrée into MacDonald's world because it does not accurately portray the thematic unity of MacDonald's lifetime message and spiritual outlook. It is always that *thematic unity*, along with individual *interest and taste,* that ought to dictate how one reads MacDonald—first time readers along with literary veterans who have been reading MacDonald for decades.

There are three major genres or categories of interest through which MacDonald's work can be approached. Most eventually intermingle their reading among all three. These are: *Theology, Realistic fiction,* and *Fairy tale and fantasy.*

THEOLOGY. MacDonald's theological writings are mostly contained in five volumes: *Unspoken Sermons, First, Second,* and *Third Series, The Hope of the Gospel,* and *The Miracles of Our Lord.* The first four titles especially represent the mother lode of MacDonald's spiritual thought. For one coming to MacDonald for the first time, however, they are *very* difficult going. Some of my own writings are much easier to start with than these volumes. I have made it one of my life's objectives to "interpret" MacDonald's writings and ideas, and assimilate them into more understandable formats and editions. Though you may eventually want to read MacDonald's original sermons, most readers find

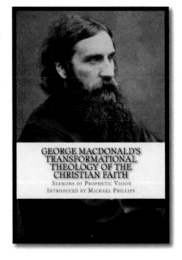

GEORGE MACDONALD'S
TRANSFORMATIONAL
THEOLOGY OF THE
CHRISTIAN FAITH
SERMONS OF PROPHETIC VISION
INTRODUCED BY MICHAEL PHILLIPS

MacDonald's ideas far easier to access and understand in the following volumes, which can be profitably read in any order:

- ❖ *George MacDonald's Spiritual Vision: An Overview*
- ❖ *Discovering the Character of God*
- ❖ *Knowing the Heart of God*
- ❖ *Your Life in Christ*
- ❖ *The Truth in Jesus*
- ❖ *George MacDonald and the Late Great Hell Debate*
- ❖ *George MacDonald's Transformational Theology of the Christian Faith.*

FAIRY TALE AND FANTASY. For readers primarily interested in fantasy, I generally follow my friend's lead and suggest *The Princess and the Goblin* as an ideal title to make acquaintance with MacDonald's fairy tale and fantasy writings. Most consider it the best of MacDonald's fairy tales. It's sequel, *The Princess and Curdie,* is much different in tone and style, as is MacDonald's best-selling book of all time, the "realistic fantasy" *At the Back of the North Wind.* The three taken together, different as they are, provide a wonderfully rich and delightful reading experience... for readers of all ages, young and old alike.

REALISTIC FICTION. Saving the best for last, I would begin by emphasizing, even to readers of theology and fairy tale, that the realistic novel was George MacDonald's primary literary vehicle. He published five volumes of theology and scriptural exposition, four fairy tales for young people, and two adult fantasies. Yet he published *thirty-one* realistic novels. MacDonald's style and overall message, his approach to life, and his enormous significance as a writer and novelist and Christian, cannot be adequately understood from his fantasy or theological writings alone. To know MacDonald accurately, and to understand his body of work, *requires* immersing oneself in his novels. MacDonald cannot be truly experienced apart from them.

My top ten MacDonald "A-list" novels, chronologically as he wrote them, are:

- ❖ *David Elginbrod* (1863)
- ❖ *Alec Forbes of Howglen* (1865)
- ❖ *Robert Falconer* (1867)
- ❖ *Malcolm* (1875)
- ❖ *Thomas Wingfold Curate* (1876)
- ❖ *The Marquis of Lossie* (1877)
- ❖ *Sir Gibbie* (1879)
- ❖ *Castle Warlock* (1881)
- ❖ *Donal Grant* (1883)
- ❖ *What's Mine's Mine* (1886)

Obviously, this is a subjective list because it is *my* list. Others would add their own favorites. Historically, however, most of these titles will be found at or near the top of any grouping of MacDonald's significant writings. The rest of his novels, as I will explain, are good—even wonderful—in their own way. Some of them are among my personal favorites. But as not everyone will be inclined to read all thirty-seven of MacDonald's fictional titles, it may be helpful to categorize them in ways that will assist readers new to MacDonald in deciding which titles they may be most interested in. Thus, identifying such an "A-list" has practical value and sets a suggested reading path that will hopefully be helpful to readers wondering where to begin.

After this brief overview, before looking at the groupings of MacDonald's novels in a little more detail, let's pause and ask another variation of the questions I mentioned that were recently put to me. Imagine at this point that someone asks me, or one of you who has been reading MacDonald for years, "I know nothing about MacDonald, but I want to know all I can. I want to read a variety of his work. I like a good story, but I also like to think about challenging spiritual ideas. I am intrigued by MacDonald not only as a storyteller but as a theologian. Where should I begin?"

Here is how I might answer.

"Read *Malcolm* or *Sir Gibbie*—I don't really care in what order. Then maybe read the other. Follow it with *Robert Falconer* or *Thomas Wingfold.* While you're dipping your feet into more fictional theological fare, I might suggest you read *George MacDonald's Spiritual Vision: An Overview.* And by then you should probably also be diving into *Discovering the Character of God* along with whatever fiction you are reading. Then it's time for some fantasy to widen your literary diet—say, *The Princess and the Goblin* or *At the Back of the North Wind.*

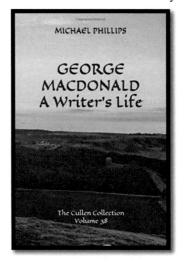

"By this time, you will either love MacDonald or will have had enough. If you love him, you probably don't need me making any more recommendations—you'll know MacDonald well enough yourself. I would only remind you not to neglect *Donal Grant, Your Life in Christ,* the other novels I've mentioned, and *Knowing the Heart of God.* Then flex your wings and fly—the whole world of MacDonald's corpus of writings awaits you! And don't discount the value of reading any or all a second or third time. When you're ready to explore MacDonald's life, I hope you might find my two biographies enjoyable— *George MacDonald Scotland's Beloved Storyteller* and *George MacDonald A Writer's Life.*"

Now let me offer an overview of MacDonald's complete fiction corpus in the six groupings of The Cullen Collection with their distinctive cover images. I will individually highlight the ten titles of my "A-list" with a little more detail.

Early Scottish Novels

- ❖ *The Portent*
- ❖ *David Elginbrod*
- ❖ *Alec Forbes of Howglen*

- ❖ *Robert Falconer*
- ❖ *Ranald Bannerman's Boyhood*
- ❖ *Gutta Percha Willie*

If any characterization fits George MacDonald as an author of realistic fiction, it would be that he was primarily a "Scottish novelist." Eleven of his novels were largely written in the Scottish dialect known as Doric. Another five are set in Scotland but without Doric. And the last in the above group, *Gutta Percha Willie may* be set in Scotland, though the locale is not identified. There are thus either sixteen or seventeen "Scottish" novels in MacDonald's fictional corpus.

David Elginbrod and *Alec Forbes of Howglen.*

David Elginbrod has the distinction of being George MacDonald's first published novel, and *Alec Forbes of Howglen* is memorable in its portrayal of MacDonald's hometown of Huntly in northern Scotland, fictionalized as Glamerton. MacDonald's son-in-law Sir Edward Troup wrote in 1924: "The essential truth of George MacDonald's boyhood will be found in *Ranald Bannerman* and in *Alec Forbes of Howglen*—not that, save in a few instances, actual incidents are related: but if you will regard Ranald and Alec as George MacDonald in boyhood, you will know what atmosphere he lived in, what were the conditions and outward circumstances of his life, and what were the influences that formed his character." To these two titles should be added *Robert Falconer* for its portrayal of the Huntly of MacDonald's youth and its many autobiographical glimpses into MacDonald's early life. These three Scottish novels published in the five years between 1863 and 1867 (*David Elginbrod, Alec Forbes,* and *Robert Falconer*) became the trilogy of works upon which George MacDonald's future reputation was built.

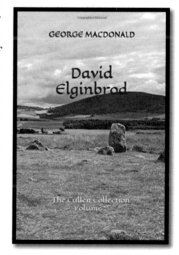

In *David Elginbrod,* MacDonald establishes a character "type" to which he will return time and again throughout his career. It is his memorable portrayal of the simple "peasant prophet" who becomes the spiritual foundation-stone of the story. Though most of the narrative follows Hugh Sutherland rather than David Elginbrod, it is David, behind the scenes, who gives focus and perspective to Hugh's development. Most of MacDonald's spiritual peasant-saints live out their quiet influence in stark contrast to worldly-wise and highly educated clergymen who consider such men (and MacDonald includes his share of women peasant-saints as well) more than a little looney. This juxtaposition of spiritual opposites is especially visible in *Donal Grant* and *Salted With Fire.* Also significant in *David Elginbrod* is the first appearance of the character of *Robert Falconer* several years before the publication of the book bearing his name.

Alec Forbes has been considered by many as George MacDonald's most skillfully crafted "pure novel," perhaps because it contains fewer digressive discussionary asides for which MacDonald's originals are well-known. Neither does MacDonald delve so deeply into Alec's spiritual psyche as he does with Falconer and Wingfold. No complex spiritual quandary drives his growth. Alec simply grows up, slowly and gradually, with ups and downs along the way, into mature manhood.

Robert Falconer

We now shift gears to a much different form of novel from George MacDonald's pen, highlighting the foremost example, along with *Thomas Wingfold Curate* which we will look at later, of what I call his "theological" novels. *Robert Falconer* is loosely linked to *David Elginbrod* which preceded it

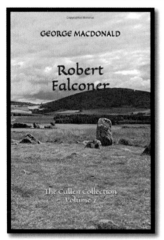

in which the character of Falconer makes his first appearance.

Critics could argue that *Robert Falconer* does not have much plot. There are no treasures, dungeons, castles, long-lost inheritances, or dramatic chases. The plot is *internal.* Falconer is engaged upon a personally imperative quest of spiritual discovery to answer the question what God is like. As always in MacDonald's books, sometimes subtly and in this case more overtly, resolving the many theological dilemmas posed by the nature and character of God looms as the imperative conundrum of life out of which all other questions in some way emerge.

Not only has *Robert Falconer* historically been the most well-known of MacDonald's realistic fiction titles, it also stands as one of MacDonald most *important* books (and no doubt its popularity stems from this as well) because of his exploration in its pages of the conundrum of hell. He does so through Falconer's probing questions about the Calvinist theology of his upbringing—and Falconer's ultimate conviction that hell exists for the purpose of final purification and repentance rather than eternal punishment. Though years earlier MacDonald had been ousted from the only pulpit he ever held for that view, it was as a result of the publication of *Robert Falconer* in the late 1860s that the charge of heresy against him became widespread. The skepticism in which MacDonald was held because of his supposed belief in what is commonly called "universalism" (a mischaracterization of his perspective of the fate of sinners after death) dogged his steps all his life, and persists in the minds of many to this day.

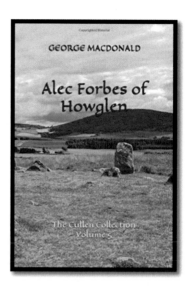

Of the six "early" Scottish novels, the three giants for which MacDonald is well known—*David Elginbrod, Alec Forbes,* and *Robert Falconer*—are all heavy with Doric. The dialect, in fact, was the chief rationale for the beginning of my editorial work on MacDonald's novels back in the 1980s. The introduction to the Cullen Collection edition of *David Elginbrod* explains what I do, and why, in updating MacDonald's novels.

The other three novels in this group are notably shorter and less well-known. *Ranald Bannerman's Boyhood* and *Gutta Percha Willie* are often considered "children's" novels, though that is not really accurate. Both chronicle the boyhood exploits of two very different young men—Ranald mischievous and always getting into scrapes, Willie one of MacDonald's almost "too good to be true" characters. Both boys, however, have fathers whom MacDonald characterizes in their own unique ways as portrayals of God himself, thus, as he nearly always manages to do, bringing the "story" into unity with the backdrop-tapestry of Fatherhood and Christlikeness that are the foundational pillars of his life's message.

That said, *The Portent* presents an anomaly, being perhaps the most *unspiritual* of MacDonald's novels. That fact may be explained in that it was actually his first written realistic novel, published in magazine form three years prior to *David Elginbrod.* It is different than any of his other books—other-worldly, spooky, a good old-fashioned "ghost story" about the Scottish second sight. It is decidedly *not* a children's story, and is sure to raise the hair on the back of the neck for even the most intrepid of readers.

Six English Novels

- ❖ *Adela Cathcart*
- ❖ *Guild Court*
- ❖ *Wilfrid Cumbermede*

- ❖ *St. George and St. Michael*
- ❖ *Mary Marston*
- ❖ *Weighed and Wanting*

It could be argued that the titles of this group are among the least known of the Cullen Collection. Yet there are gems to be found here as in all MacDonald's writing. The two last titles are especially noteworthy as featuring women in the leading roles (along with *The Vicar's Daughter* and *The Flight of the Shadow*) and dealing with many so-called "women's themes." Both Mary of the book bearing her name and Hester of *Weighed and Wanting*, face dilemmas and decisions about work and career, marriage, and Christian ministry. MacDonald's insight and sensitivity in telling the stories of these two virtuous women is all the more remarkable in that he wrote these books more than a century-and-a-quarter ago! He was ahead of his time in many ways, including his keen understanding of women's changing role in society.

Guild Court, as probably MacDonald's least-known realistic novel, is subtitled "A London Story," a description which characterizes it to perfection. MacDonald introduces a range of unique characters whose lives are intertwined in fascinating ways. Then we watch them live and interact and grow. Some grow better, some grow worse. The two principal lead players in the drama, Lucy and Thomas—along with another of MacDonald's virtuous and stellar ministers, Mr. Fuller—though unknown to many readers, are sure to take their places in the gallery of MacDonald's memorable fictional creations.

The remaining three titles are so decidedly unique, that it will probably be most helpful for those interested to read the descriptions that follow in the next section.

Two English Trilogies

- ❖ *Annals of a Quiet Neighbourhood*
- ❖ *The Seaboard Parish*
- ❖ *The Vicar's Daughter*

- ❖ *Thomas Wingfold Curate*
- ❖ *Paul Faber Surgeon*
- ❖ *There and Back*

Though George MacDonald was not a writer of what today we would call series fiction, he did in fact write two trilogies. Both are set in England, and both are built upon the lives of clergymen—Harry Walton of what is called the "Marshmallows trilogy, and Thomas Wingfold, who, though the three books are independent stories, plays a central role in the three latter titles.

The three earlier volumes are written in the first person (the first two by fictional narrator-minister Walton, the third by his fictional daughter), and relate the daily goings-on of parish and family life. They are somewhat thin of plot, yet the first two in particular are filled with MacDonald's wonderful insights and reflections. Some of his most memorable quotes about God and the spiritual life are found in their pages.

Thomas Wingfold Curate

A foremost example of what I call his "theological" novels, Wingfold's story shares many similarities with *Robert Falconer*. In purpose and style, the two books are very similar. The plots in both cases are *internal:* in Wingfold's case, to answer the question what it means to be saved.

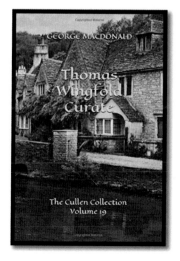

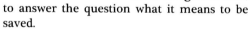
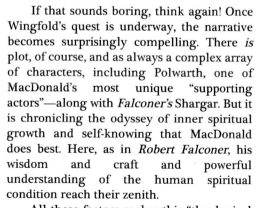

If that sounds boring, think again! Once Wingfold's quest is underway, the narrative becomes surprisingly compelling. There *is* plot, of course, and as always a complex array of characters, including Polwarth, one of MacDonald's most unique "supporting actors"—along with *Falconer's* Shargar. But it is chronicling the odyssey of inner spiritual growth and self-knowing that MacDonald does best. Here, as in *Robert Falconer*, his wisdom and craft and powerful understanding of the human spiritual condition reach their zenith.

All these factors makes this "theological novel" among MacDonald's most popular of all time. *Thomas Wingfold* has always been among the most well-received of my edited editions of MacDonald's works.

The second and third "Wingfold novels" pick up where Wingfold's personal journey of faith left off. MacDonald continues his exploration of the nature of belief, first in the life of atheist Paul Faber, then in the lives of two of his most memorable and thoughtful young people—Barbara Wilder and Richard Tuke of *There and Back*. These two Wingfold "sequels" explore many salvationary themes—sin, goodness, repentance, hypocrisy, and the role of intellectual honesty in spirituality—not merely with insight and wisdom, but with logical and thoughtful profundity.

It is in *There and Back* that MacDonald poses one of the truly transformational queries upon which all life could be said to revolve—what kind of God do we believe in? So pivotal do I consider MacDonald's statement in the book, "everything depend[s] on the kind of God believed in," that I identified the imperative of "Knowing God Truly" as the first and foundational principle in *George MacDonald's Spiritual Vision, An Introductory Overview.* As he wrote in *Unspoken Sermons Second Series,* "How have we learned Christ? It ought to be a startling thought, that we may have learned him wrong. That must be far worse than not to have learned him at all: his place is occupied by a false Christ…Good souls many will one day be horrified at the things they now believe of God. (From "The Truth in Jesus" and "Self-Denial")

The three volumes of the Wingfold trilogy provide a spiritually meaty full-course apologetics meal based upon the questions: *Who is God and what is he like, what is the nature of faith, and what does true belief really mean?*

The Scottish Masterworks

- *Malcolm*
- *The Marquis of Lossie*
- *Sir Gibbie*

- *Castle Warlock*
- *Donal Grant*
- *What's Mine's Mine*

The zenith of George MacDonald's writing career was reached in the mid to late 1870s and early 1880s. During the period between 1875 and 1886, a staggering twenty books were published, including these six, which by any standard are among his very best.

Malcolm and *The Marquis of Lossie.*

The doublet telling the story of Scottish fisherman Malcolm is unquestionably MacDonald's most riveting and skillfully crafted plot-driven "story." Its characters are among MacDonald's best, and the sheer art of fictional excellence make it unrivaled among his books. The correspondence to place also distinguishes these volumes. Set in the northern Scottish fishing village of Cullen (fictionalized as Portlossie) of the 1860s and 1870s (the approximate time-setting for most of MacDonald's novels), one visiting Cullen and its environs truly feels that he or she has stepped back a century and a half *into* the story. In some ways little has changed. MacDonald's descriptions in the pages of *Malcolm* remain vivid portrayals of village and coastline as they still exist today. This gives the books a palpable *reality* all their own.

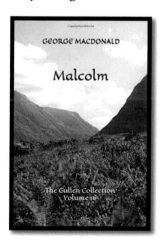

GEORGE MACDONALD

Malcolm

The Cullen Collection
Volume 16

For its superior plot, exquisite and diverse range of characters, and reality of place, I nearly always recommend my Cullen Collection edition of *Malcolm* as a "first read" (in the absence of other factors) for one coming to MacDonald's novels for the first time. The *Malcolm* doublet is equally important in establishing the thematic unity of MacDonald's lifetime spiritual orientation of the Fatherhood of God, Christlikeness of character, and obedience to the commands of Jesus. The plot, characters, relationships, and setting weave together a complex and many-hued tapestry in which these undergirding spiritual themes emerge as backdrop to the whole. *Malcolm* and *The Marquis of Lossie* thus exhibit MacDonald's mastery of the fictional craft, as well as solidifying a spiritual foundation for his entire corpus of work in all its genres.

Sir Gibbie and Donal Grant.

Second to *Malcolm*, I point potential readers nearly as often to the magical tale of wee Sir Gibbie. Also powerful of plot, *Sir Gibbie* is infused with what is almost the mythical nature of the homeless waif who is its central character and the source of its enduring power. I know of no other character in fiction exactly like Gibbie, which explains why his story has been a lifetime favorite among all MacDonald's books for so many.

The hues of Christlikeness that provide the tapestry backdrop for all MacDonald's novels shine out with special radiance in *Sir Gibbie* and its sequel *Donal Grant.* Orphan Gibbie *without* a father discovers his true Father, while his best friend Donal, a young man growing up with MacDonald's prototypical image of wonderful parents, discovers with Gibbie the essence of true childship. The journeys of growth of both young men, so different of outward circumstance, lead to the same childship-obedience in the end.

To say more about Gibbie and his story might too easily spoil the reading experience awaiting those who have yet to discover it. I will only add this from my introduction to the Cullen Collection edition:

"Is *Sir Gibbie* 'myth'…Is it poetry? Is it fantasy? Is it music?

"Or does Gibbie's magic spring from MacDonald's having simultaneously captured the essence of all four? The story tugs at us, the myth calls forth eternity in our spirits, the poetry moves us, the fantasy delights our imaginations, while all along the music makes our hearts sing.

"*Sir Gibbie* is all this and more.

"Through the title character of wee Gibbie, we do not merely meet a mythical, musical, poetical child of God—we meet MacDonald himself, and, through Gibbie, see through MacDonald's eyes into the essence of spirituality."

Though *Sir Gibbie* has generally overshadowed *Donal Grant* through the years, the story of Gibbie's friend (which has the distinction of being MacDonald's longest book—786 pages in its original) has always been one of my personal favorites. Its plot is far more leisurely, and the discussionary digressions more numerous. As a result, it is not what some might call a "page-turner" (though its climax is probably the most dramatic and scary sequence in MacDonald's novels!) But the *character* of Donal is superbly drawn. I often say that I want to be Malcolm and Donal when I grow up. For almost forty years, these two young men of MacDonald's creation have been role models to me.

Castle Warlock and What's Mine's Mine.

Something we have not yet talked about in connection with MacDonald's novels is Scotland itself. The homeland of MacDonald's birth is in a sense a central "character" in many of his best books. It is no accident that nine of my ten "A-list" titles (*Thomas Wingfold* as the sole exception) are set in Scotland. In the Preface to his *Anthology* of quotes from MacDonald's sermons, C.S. Lewis writes: "All that is best in his novels carries us back to that 'kaleyard' world of granite and heather, of bleaching greens beside burns that look as if they flowed not with water but with stout, to the thudding of wooden machinery, the oatcakes, the fresh milk, the pride, the poverty, and the passionate love of hard-won learning."

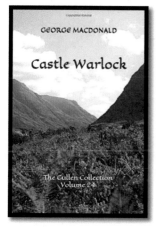

MacDonald's two most graphically typical "highland" novels are *Castle Warlock* and *What's Mine's Mine*. Along with *Malcolm, Marquis, Gibbie,* and *Donal,* they round out "The Scottish Masterworks" of the Cullen Collection. Both these titles are almost entirely set in the highlands and do not shift in and out of other locales as does *Sir Gibbie* and *The Marquis of Lossie.* Both, too, are set in the midst of circumstances depicting the declining fortunes of families who have made the highlands their home for generations. The Highland Clearances of the late eighteenth and nineteenth centuries brought wholesale change throughout the north and west of Scotland. MacDonald explores the impact of these changes on the fortunes of the families Warlock and Macruadh. Uniting spiritual themes and plot in MacDonald's usually skillful fashion, both Cosmo Warlock and Alister Macruadh must each face the agonizing personal pain of relinquishment, laying all they hold dear on the altar of sacrifice even as they see the land they love so passionately slipping from their grasp.

The Short Novels

- ❖ *Home Again*
- ❖ *The Elect Lady*
- ❖ *A Rough Shaking*
- ❖ *The Flight of the Shadow*

- ❖ *Heather and Snow*
- ❖ *Salted With Fire*
- ❖ *Far Above Rubies*

As George MacDonald's writing life gradually wound down, though his output remained prodigious, his novels became noticeably shorter. The final seven realistic novels that closed out his career—four Scottish, three English—represent a potpourri of unique styles, settings, and themes.

Home Again and *The Elect Lady* are often linked simply because of their similar length and near simultaneous writing. Otherwise, however, they are unrelated—the one a prodigal tale, the other a thematic parable of the church.

A Rough Shaking, though often called a "children's story" is in reality more complex than such a characterization reveals. Overlooked by many critics because Clare—as is said of several of MacDonald's characters—is "too good to be true," his quest after fatherhood, and his determination to be "good," links Clare's story to the very best in all MacDonald's books.

The Flight of the Shadow is different in flavor than most of MacDonald's other novels, and without the deep level of spiritual import we are used to from him. I find a similarity to *The Portent,* though others may not. The book represents another first-person female-narrator story.

MacDonald's realistic fictional career reached its conclusion with three more Scottish tales. *Heather and Snow* and *Salted With Fire* are both written in heavy Doric dialect and set near MacDonald's hometown of Huntly. The depiction of the highlands in *Heather and Snow* ranks as among MacDonald's most vivid. And in *Salted With Fire* we encounter one of MacDonald's most memorable "peasant-prophets" in the person of John MacLear. Written literally but months before the stroke that finally stilled MacDonald's pen, *Far Above Rubies,* a short "novella" of a mere 25,000 words, though in the guise of fiction, represents MacDonald's poignant final retrospective as he gazes back at the beginning of his own writing career.

Full Length Fantasies

- ❖ Phantastes
- ❖ At the Back of the North Wind
- ❖ The Princess and the Goblin
- ❖ The Wise Woman
- ❖ The Princess and Curdie
- ❖ Lilith

"It must be more than thirty years ago that I bought...the Everyman edition of Phantastes. A few hours later I knew that I had crossed a great frontier."—C.S. Lewis"

"At The Back of the North Wind...seems to stand, in its mystery and simplicity...far above its fellows...George MacDonald gives us the two worlds co-existent; not here and there, but both here and now. And its three great persons, North Wind, Diamond the boy, and Diamond the cab-horse, speak more wisdom than will ever be spoken about them."—Ronald MacDonald

"I for one can really testify to a book that has made a difference to my whole existence, which helped me to see things in a certain way...Of all the stories I have read...it remains the most real, the most realistic, in the exact sense of the phrase the most like life. It is called The Princess and the Goblin, and is by George MacDonald."—G.K. Chesterton

"This is a magical tale...The Lost Princess catches up the reader by the sheer magic of its story and takes him along through a series of adventures that are whimsical, beautiful, heart-rending. Impossible? Perhaps not quite. It all depends on the definition of possible."—Elizabeth Yates

"Curdie is one of the true 'role-model" characters in MacDonald's fantasies...What powerful insight is contained in his exclamation, "I must mind what I am about." In seven simple words, MacDonald has unlocked the key to the universe...This passage, as Curdie is empowered for his mission, represents one of the most significant moments in all my reading of MacDonald. I consider it a true mountaintop in all MacDonald's corpus. I have never looked at people the same again (including myself), nor the entire human drama, since I first read it forty-five years ago. I think it was this passage, along with that concerning the impact of choice upon 'the central part of us' from MacDonald's protégé Lewis, that began my lifelong quest to focus my spiritual attention on trying to do what Jesus said, and thereby mind what I was about."—Michael Phillips

"George MacDonald's books must tell us more of his life than could any biography; and we must look to the most notable of his last works for the crowning expressions of himself and his life...The way in which my father first wrote Lilith in 1890 is important. He was possessed by a feeling...that it was a mandate direct from God...I lay all this stress on the importance of Lilith...for it was...the majestic thought of his old age."—Greville MacDonald

A Chronological Listing with Brief Descriptions
George MacDonald fiction with prominent 19ᵗʰ century covers

Phantastes—*The Cullen Collection Volume 1*

George MacDonald's first major fiction work, in MacDonald's words "a sort of fairy tale for grown people," *Phantastes* was published in 1858. This unusual fantasy, subtitled a "fairie romance," is one of MacDonald's most mysterious and esoteric titles. The book's narrator, Anodos, enters Fairy Land through a mysterious old wooden secretary. From that beginning, he embarks on a dream-like series of encounters that follow the form of an epic quest, though the purpose and destination of his journey remain obscure and are never fully clarified. Two volumes of poetry prior to this had set MacDonald apart as a talented young author to watch in England's literary circles. Sales of *Phantastes*, however, proved a disappointment, and thus MacDonald ultimately turned to the writing of realistic fiction in the 1860s. When young atheist C.S. Lewis discovered *Phantastes* in 1916, within a few hours he said he knew he "had crossed a great frontier." MacDonald's unusual fantasy set Lewis on the road toward his eventual conversion to Christianity, and forever after he referred to MacDonald as his "master." In spite of its poor initial reception among Victorian readers, Lewis's affection for it established *Phantastes* as one of MacDonald's most enduring and studied works in literary and academic circles. This new edition is one of six fantasy titles in *The Cullen Collection* that has not been edited or updated in any way and is reproduced exactly in its original text.

David Elginbrod—*The Cullen Collection Volume 2*

George MacDonald's first realistic novel, *David Elginbrod,* was published in 1863. Unable to get his poetry and fantasy published, one of MacDonald's publishers remarked, "I tell you, Mr. MacDonald, if you would but write *novels*, you would find all the publishers saving up to buy them of you. Nothing but fiction pays." Eventually MacDonald decided to try his hand at realistic fiction, and his publisher's words proved prophetic—within a few years publishers indeed were lining up to buy his books. The immediate success of *David Elginbrod* launched MacDonald's career as one of the preeminent Victorian novelists of his day. Partially set in MacDonald's homeland of northern Scotland, the story of Hugh Sutherland and Margaret Elginbrod is replete with the dialect and thorough "Scottishness" that became MacDonald's trademark. The story takes the characters into the eerie world of the occult and spiritualism that so fascinated Victorian readers. This new edition streamlines the occasionally ponderous Victorian narrative style, and updates the thick Doric brogue into readable English.

The Portent—*The Cullen Collection Volume 3*

The Portent was originally written for magazine serialization several years prior to its release in book form in 1864. Shorter than most of MacDonald's novels, this spooky tale of the Scottish "second sight" is a thorough spine-tingling ghost story worthy of the twilight zone. MacDonald's love of mysterious old castles and libraries plays a significant role in the story and is found in many of his books. In *The Portent*, first person narrator Duncan Campbell is engaged as tutor in a large mansion. There he falls under the spell of somnambulist Lady Alice, who is trapped between the worlds of wakefulness and sleep. About this title, MacDonald's son Greville commented: "The story is different from almost any other of his books. It is weird, yet strangely convincing, and has no touch of the didactic." Because of its mystical flavor, *The Portent* is often linked with MacDonald's earlier *Phantastes*. Though the books are completely different, *The Portent* yet contains elements that appeal to readers of MacDonald's fantasy writings, and thus spans the genres of both fantasy and realistic fiction.

Adela Cathcart—*The Cullen Collection Volume 4*

Reminiscent of Chaucer's *Canterbury Tales,* MacDonald's attempt to package a collection of short stories in the guise of a novel is built around a group of friends and neighbors sharing stories in hopes of lifting the spirits of young Adela Cathcart who is suffering from a mysterious illness. Early in his career, MacDonald was trying different genres and storytelling methods, and this is a prime example of his creative experimentation. First published in 1864, the included stories changed with a new edition in 1882. Some of MacDonald's well-known short stories made their first appearance in one of the two editions. This new publication includes the stories from both original editions.

Alec Forbes of Howglen—*The Cullen Collection Volume 5*

Released in 1865 as the second of his major Scottish novels, many consider *Alec Forbes of Howglen* George MacDonald's most uniformly cohesive work of fiction. Intensely Scottish in flavor, like its predecessor *David Elginbrod,* the thick Doric dialect of much of the novel was relished by Victorians. Set in MacDonald's hometown of Huntly, this story of Alec Forbes and Annie Anderson contains many autobiographical glimpses of MacDonald's own boyhood, capturing the delights of youth and the anguish of first loves. While preserving the flavor of MacDonald's original, this updated edition translates the Scottish dialect, in which most of MacDonald's Scottish stories are written, into readable English.

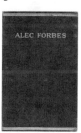

Annals of a Quiet Neighbourhood—*The Cullen Collection Volume 6*

MacDonald's first major English novel, published in 1867, was set in the village of Arundel on the downs south of London near the south channel coast. It was the site of MacDonald's first and only pastorate as a newly married minister in 1851-53. This book is wonderfully descriptive of the region, with autobiographical hints of MacDonald's outlook as a young pastor. The story chronicles the daily life of one of MacDonald's fictionalized "ideal ministers"—perhaps as a portrayal of the shepherd-pastor MacDonald had himself hoped to be—the *Annals* proved one of his most popular novels. First released in the *Sunday Magazine,* which was intended for "Sabbath reading," *Annals of a Quiet Neighbourhood* was quickly published in numerous book editions, and contributed in a significant way to MacDonald's growing popularity in America. Though less spine-riveting of

plot, the three volumes of the "Marshmallows Trilogy" spawned by *Annals* provide some of MacDonald's most homiletic and deeply spiritual writings.

Robert Falconer—*The Cullen Collection Volume 7*

In George MacDonald's most well-known novel, published in 1868, the quest of young Robert Falconer for his father becomes a parallel quest to break free from the oppressive Calvinist theology of his grandmother. As he struggles to come to terms with the strict orthodoxy prevalent in Scotland for two centuries, the doctrine of hell looms as the great stumbling block in Robert's mind. His lifelong search reveals to Robert the groundbreaking truth that hell is remedial not punitive, designed to produce ultimate repentance not everlasting punishment. This highly autobiographical work offers a rare glimpse into MacDonald's own youthful quandaries, and a window into the development of his faith, which would turn generations toward the Fatherhood of a loving God. After the book's publication (which Queen Victoria gave to each of her grandsons), as a result of the bold themes running through the narrative, MacDonald came to be considered a "universalist" and "heretic" in some circles—grievous mischaracterizations that persist to this day. This new edition streamlines the occasionally ponderous Victorian narrative style, and updates the thick Doric brogue into readable English.

Guild Court—*The Cullen Collection Volume 8*

Following on the heels of Robert Falconer's hugely influential and controversial story, *Guild Court*, written concurrently with *Falconer* and published the same year, is one of MacDonald's lesser known novels. A love story set in London, its portrait of many intertwining and quirky lives in and around a city court is perhaps the most Dickens-like of MacDonald's novels. Though not a book that enjoyed such widespread circulation as his others, *Guild Court* yet contains many of the signature tunes found throughout George MacDonald's fictional corpus, and presents a powerful story of repentance, forgiveness, and reconciliation.

The Seaboard Parish—*The Cullen Collection Volume 9*

The publication in 1868 of this sequel to *Annals of a Quiet Neighbourhood* capped off one of George MacDonald's most productive years with a third major fiction work following *Robert Falconer* and *Guild Court*. Set in the Cornwall seaside town of Bude and inspired by a MacDonald family holiday a few years earlier, this novel continues the leisurely pastoral pace of minister Harry Walton's family. Like *Annals of a Quiet Neighbourhood*, it was first written for "Sabbath reading" in the *Sunday Magazine*. Almost taking the form of a "family diary," *A Seaboard Parish* is yet rich with spiritual insight and wisdom.

At the Back of the North Wind—*The Cullen Collection Volume 10*

Historically, *At the Back of the North Wind* ranks as George MacDonald's most well-known and enduring book, the haunting tale of little Diamond, a simple London cabman's son and his dreamy encounters with the mysterious, wise, powerful, comforting, and occasionally frightening lady known as North Wind. Their eerie nighttime adventures have captivated readers old and young ever since the book's publication in 1871. It has been published in more editions than any of MacDonald's works, and ranks as one of the few (perhaps only) title of MacDonald's that has likely never been out of print. Its skillfully woven intermingling of realism and fantasy set MacDonald apart as a writer of uniqueness and distinction in the early 1870s as his reputation widened. This edition for *The Cullen Collection* is unedited in any way.

Ranald Bannerman's Boyhood—*The Cullen Collection Volume 11*

Released in 1871 after *At the Back of the North Wind*, MacDonald's first realistic "young readers" novel follows the boyhood adventures of Ranald Bannerman up to the moment in his teens when he realizes that he is "not a man." Thus begins his growth into *true* manhood. MacDonald's editorship of the highly popular magazine *Good Words for the Young* in the late 1860s and early 1870s resulted in five young-reader stories, starting with *At the Back of the North Wind*, and continuing with *Ranald Bannerman's Boyhood* and *The Princess and the Goblin* in

succession. Set in and around MacDonald's Scottish hometown of Huntly, many of young Ranald's escapades, as in most of MacDonald's Scots stories, are autobiographical. Ranald Bannerman fictionally presents the lighter, occasionally mischievous, side of MacDonald's boyhood.

The Princess and the Goblin—*The Cullen Collection Volume 12*

As editor of the magazine *Good Words for the Young*, MacDonald had a ready audience for "fairy tale" and "children's" stories, and produced some of his most famous titles during this period of his writing life. The third of his stories for the magazine, *The Princess and the Goblin*, published in 1872, is universally acclaimed as MacDonald's best pure fairy tale, and has been enchanting readers for well over a century. This story of princess Irene, her mysterious ageless namesake "grandmother," and miner's son Curdie surely provided

inspiration for C.S. Lewis's *Chronicles of Narnia*. G.K. Chesterton wrote of it in 1924, "I...can really testify to a book that has made a difference to my whole existence, which has helped me to see...a vision of things...so real....Of all the stories I have read...it remains the most real, the most realistic, in the exact sense of the phrase the most like life. It is called *The Princess and the Goblin*, and it is by George MacDonald." This edition for *The Cullen Collection* is unedited in any way.

Wilfrid Cumbermede—*The Cullen Collection Volume 13*

This dark realistic novel is somewhat puzzling in MacDonald's corpus of more uplifting works. Some of its disconcerting themes grew out of George and Louisa MacDonald's friendship with author John Ruskin during a troubled time in the latter's life. Some of the descriptive portions contained within this narrative, especially of the Swiss Alps, are among MacDonald's finest.

The Vicar's Daughter—*The Cullen Collection Volume 14*

The Vicar's Daughter, the 1872 sequel to *The Seaboard Parish,* follows the early married life of one of Harry Walton's (fictional narrator of *Annals of a Quiet Neighbourhood*) daughters. This third book in The Marshmallows Trilogy is representative of the rising interest women were taking in Victorian society. Written in the first person in the fictional guise of female authorship, its characterization of MacDonald's friend and patron Lady Noel Byron is one of the noteworthy elements of the book.

Gutta Percha Willie—*The Cullen Collection Volume 15*

While still editing the magazine *Good Words for the Young,* MacDonald wrote this second "boy's novel," unconnected with but written for a similar audience as Ranald Bannerman's story. Inventive young Willie Macmichael turns everything about him to creative uses, hungrily learning from the grown-ups around him, prompting MacDonald's subtitle, "The Working Genius." Though one of MacDonald's lesser-known titles, I comment in the introduction: "MacDonald's strongest and most eternal contribution to the world lies in the realm of *spiritual practicality.* Willie epitomizes the *practicality* of growing into one's place in God's general business. This story therefore deserves to be considered one of MacDonald's memorable portrayals of that eternal imperative. I love this book!" *Gutta Percha Willie* was MacDonald's only book published in 1873, released while he was on a lecture tour in America.

Malcolm—*The Cullen Collection Volume 16*

This towering 1875 novel, set in the Scottish fishing village of Cullen, is considered by many as George MacDonald's fictional masterwork. The intricate tale is more true to place than any of MacDonald's books. As Malcolm is drawn into the web of secrets surrounding majestic Lossie House, with the marquis of Lossie and his tempestuous daughter Florimel at the center of them, we meet some of MacDonald's most memorable characters. Through them Malcolm must unravel many mysteries that hang over the town and its people—and himself! The Scottish dialect is more impenetrable than in many of MacDonald's other Scottish novels, and has been translated into readable English in this newly updated edition. I call it a "masterpiece of plot, drama, mystery, characterization, and spiritual depth," it was *Malcolm* which in the 1970s set me on my life's-work to acquaint the world with MacDonald's forgotten legacy through new editions of MacDonald's work.

I believe that *Malcolm* is always an ideal choice for new readers to begin a deeper acquaintance with MacDonald, especially as it is set in the locale from which *The Cullen Collection* of new editions derives its name. My lengthy introduction sets Malcolm's story into the context of MacDonald's two 1870s visits to Cullen, and also provides readers new to the works of MacDonald with a historical overview of the Scotsman's writing and significance.

The Wise Woman: A Parable—*The Cullen Collection Volume 17*

This shorter fairy tale "The Lost Princess" or "A Double Story" (by which titles it was also published), tells the story of spoiled Princess Rosamond, and a mysterious wise woman whom she meets in the forest, and who continues to come to her in different guises which the princess does not always recognize. Considered by some as one of MacDonald's "short stories" rather than a novel, this edition includes MacDonald's insightful essay, "The Fantastic Imagination." This edition of *The Wise Woman* for *The Cullen Collection* is unedited.

St. George and St. Michael—*The Cullen Collection Volume 18*

This unique novel in the MacDonald collection, his only true historical novel, is set during the mid-17 century English civil war. MacDonald's use of the idiom and stylistic old-English of the post-Shakespearean era make this a slow read in the original. It is greatly enhanced in this new and updated edition. *St. George and St. Michael* is an enchanting love story that offers a unique and balanced perspective on a tumultuous and conflicting era in British history.

Thomas Wingfold Curate—*The Cullen Collection Volume 19*

The character of Thomas Wingfold is introduced in this preeminent of George MacDonald's English novels, a young curate suddenly brought face-to-face with the hypocrisy of having sought the pulpit as a profession rather than a spiritual calling. Wingfold's prayerful journey into faith highlights MacDonald's most powerful "theological novel." We also meet the dwarf Joseph Polwarth, Wingfold's spiritual mentor and one of MacDonald's most memorable humble apologists for truth. The depth and poignancy of Wingfold's quest makes this 1876 publication one of MacDonald's best-loved works. I rank *Thomas Wingfold Curate* near the apex of MacDonald's corpus, among my personal favorites along with *Malcolm, Sir Gibbie,* and *Donal Grant.*

The Marquis of Lossie—*The Cullen Collection Volume 20*

This 1877 sequel to *Malcolm* begins where the first volume of the doublet left off, at Lossie House in Cullen's fictionalized Portlossie. Soon thereafter Malcolm travels to London to rescue Florimel from the harmful influences of duplicitous friends who do not have her best interests in mind. Whisking her away from London, Malcolm's and Florimel's return to the north coast of Scotland brings to a stirring climax the divergent threads of mystery and intrigue woven through this triumphant literary tapestry. It is a classic Victorian romance, complete with rogues, inheritances, castles, and of course true love. Of *The Marquis of Lossie,* I have said, "Escaping a common pitfall of sequels not measuring up to the level of excellence of their predecessor, MacDonald crafts an equally engaging, and in some ways an even heightened dramatic crescendo to Malcolm's story. With the setting so altered, this is a spectacular creative achievement."

Paul Faber Surgeon—*The Cullen Collection Volume 21*

In this second of the Thomas Wingfold "trilogy," atheist Paul Faber, encountering spiritually invigorated minister Wingfold, finds himself

unexpectedly drawn into his own unwelcome quest for truth.
Now it is Wingfold—assisted by Polwarth—sharing his
newfound faith with both Paul Faber and Juliet Meredith,
whose past secrets draw them together yet also threaten to tear
them apart. In the introduction, I comment, "Of MacDonald's
unique characters, one stands alone—Paul Faber, the surgeon
of fictional Glaston. He is the only skeptic, unbeliever, and
atheist to take the spotlight as a featured title character. The
relationship between Thomas Wingfold, the curate, and his
atheist friend…gives us a vivid picture of George MacDonald's
perspective on how the life of Christ is most effectively communicated into an
unbelieving world…It is conveyed by the way Christians *live*."

Sir Gibbie—*The Cullen Collection Volume 22*

One of the true high marks in George MacDonald's literary
career was reached with the publication in 1879 of *Sir Gibbie*,
the captivating story of a mute orphan with an angel's heart
set in the highlands of Scotland. Every MacDonald reader has
his or her favorite, but it is safe to say that *Sir Gibbie* is near
the top of the list for lovers of fairy tale, poetry, and novels
alike. The character of "wee Sir Gibbie" mysteriously
embodies hints from the land of "faerie," and his soul is poetry
personified. MacDonald's storytelling genius here rises to
heights as soaring as the mountain of Glashgar where Gibbie roams barefoot
with the sheep, amid earthquake and flood. It was this book that captured
authoress Elizabeth Yates' imagination and prompted her 1963 edition of *Sir
Gibbie,* which in turn led to my updated editions that helped inaugurate the
MacDonald renaissance of the 1980s. If one could choose but one MacDonald
novel to read, many would say it should be *Sir Gibbie.* Following Elizabeth
Yates' example, I again translate the difficult Doric dialect of MacDonald's
original into more accessible English.

Mary Marston—*The Cullen Collection Volume 23*

One of MacDonald's lengthy and powerful, but not widely
studied, novels, *Mary Marston* is the only book in the
MacDonald corpus with a woman featured in the title role. As
one of MacDonald's many strong and memorable leading
ladies, Mary exemplifies a life of dedication to Christ, self-
sacrifice, and obedience to parents. We encounter here a
touching portrayal of that earthly relationship so dear to
MacDonald's heart, because it so embodied man's relationship
with God—the relationship between fathers and their sons and
daughters. Of the diverse range of characters found within the
pages of this novel, I wrote in the introduction, "Taken together, their
individual lives make fascinating reading. They are so diverse, sometimes so
petty and foolish, their intertwining relationships so humorous at times…we
observe human growth at work…always progressing in one direction or the
other—sometimes straight, sometimes crooked. It is a diverse character mix in
many shades of gray…containing diverse character flaws without easy
resolutions. It is one of the most *real* array of characters in the MacDonald
corpus."

Castle Warlock—*The Cullen Collection Volume 24*

Thematically linked to *Mary Marston* which preceded it, MacDonald here
poignantly depicts the father-son relationship as he had earlier that of father
and daughter. MacDonald's storytelling power again returns to the highlands

of Scotland, setting his narrative in the hills south of Huntly. We encounter vivid descriptions of that wild terrain, including snowstorms, summer joys, harvests, along with MacDonald's trademark mysteries, inheritances, treasures, and, of course, romance. *Castle Warlock* is one of the most thoroughly Scottish of MacDonald's novels, and is a favorite with many for its spiritual, relational, and natural splendor. *Castle Warlock* is unique among MacDonald's titles, being first published in America in 1881, six months in advance of its British counterpart of 1882. This new edition streamlines the occasionally ponderous Victorian narrative style, and updates the thick Doric brogue into readable English.

The Princess and Curdie—*The Cullen Collection Volume 25*

This story is a sequel to *The Princess and the Goblin*, but this second "Curdie" installment, published in 1882, is far more than a mere "children's story." The themes and linguistic style of *The Princess and Curdie* are considerably more advanced, and the depth of its spiritual analogies extensive in subtlety and scope. After being thrust into the rose-fire, the discerning gift of Curdie's hand to know toward what any man or woman is growing (beast or child), is one of MacDonald's most memorable, though chilling, images. It is a theme that became profoundly illuminated in later years by MacDonald's spiritual protégé C.S. Lewis, when he wrote in *Mere Christianity*, "Every time you make a choice you are turning the central part of you, the part of you that chooses, into something a little different from what it was before. And taking your life as a whole, with all your innumerable choices, all your life long you are slowly turning this central thing either into a heavenly creature or a hellish creature." Lewis's words embody a truth that emerges directly out of Curdie's story. This edition for *The Cullen Collection* is unedited in any way.

Weighed and Wanting—*The Cullen Collection Volume 26*

This 1882 story of a dysfunctional family features another of MacDonald's memorable female protagonists. Reminiscent of Mary St. John of *Robert Falconer*, Hester Raymount chooses a single life of ministry among London's downtrodden (whose character and work were inspired by MacDonald friend and social activist Octavia Hill), and, like Mary Marston, uses her musical gifts to further that ministry. The poignant character of Hester's brother Mark brings to life a moving portrait of MacDonald's own son Maurice, whom he and Louisa lost at the age of fifteen but a short while before this book was written.

Donal Grant—*The Cullen Collection Volume 27*

This magnificent 1883 sequel to *Sir Gibbie*, and MacDonald's longest book, is a novel with everything—a Gothic castle with hidden rooms and passageways, good guys and bad guys, mysteries and inheritances. and poignant yet bittersweet love. Little does Gibbie's friend Donal realize what he is in for when he takes a tutoring job at mysterious Castle Graham! Woven throughout, of course, are many signature tunes of MacDonald's wisdom and spiritual insight, including one of C.S. Lewis's favorite MacDonald lines, that God is "easy to please but hard to satisfy." Along with *Malcolm*, *Donal Grant* presents one of MacDonald's most intricate and riveting plots, led by another of his stellar characters of virtue and truth. Its massive length, however (786 pages in the original), difficult Scots dialect, and numerous digressive tangents, illustrate better than any MacDonald title the need for condensed contemporary editions. *Donal Grant* is unique in the MacDonald corpus as being originally released in two different editions in Great Britain and America. This updated edition, which I rank as one of my favorite MacDonald titles, epitomizes the value and significance of *The Cullen Collection* in bringing the fiction of George MacDonald alive for new generations.

What's Mine's Mine—*The Cullen Collection Volume 28*

This Scottish masterpiece of 1886 contains wonderfully descriptive passages of the Scottish highlands. The story centers around two families—the English Palmers and that of clan chief Alister Macruadh—and Mr. Palmer's cruel removal of Clan Ruadh from its traditional lands. This portrait of the Highland Clearances poignantly captures how and why the clan way of life disappeared from the highlands in the 18- and 19- centuries. One of MacDonald's signature tunes, God's revelation in nature, is woven throughout the narrative. Along with *Robert Falconer, What's Mine's Mine* also offers insight into MacDonald's controversial views on the afterlife. The pointed discussions between Calvinist Mrs. Macruadh and her sons Alister and Ian are memorable indeed. In spite of its highland flavor, this intensely Scottish tale did not employ the local dialect, which at the time was primarily Gaelic.

Home Again—*The Cullen Collection Volume 29*

One of MacDonald's smaller novels in length, and neither so ambitious of scope or depth, *Home Again* from 1887 is loosely based on the prodigal son parable. It is the oft-told tale of an ambitious young man who thinks too highly of himself, falls under the spell of a duplicitous young woman, and must find his way "home." Though less complex than MacDonald's lengthier novels, everything he wrote radiated light. Even in its simplicity, this story of a young poet and his return to his father and his roots has many touching moments, with MacDonald's wisdom woven throughout the characters and relationships.

The Elect Lady—*The Cullen Collection Volume 30*

Although one of MacDonald's lesser-known books, *The Elect Lady*, published in 1888, stands out for the memorable relationship of godliness, trust, honesty, and humility between three children—Andrew and Sandy Ingram and their friend Dawtie—whose growth into adulthood MacDonald follows with simple yet moving power. Their relationships provide the foundation for MacDonald's wisdom to shine forth on the nature and purpose of the church, climaxing in the memorable pronouncement from Andrew's mouth: "I don't believe that Jesus cares much for what is called the visible church. But he cares with his very Godhead for those who do as he tells them."

A Rough Shaking—*The Cullen Collection Volume 31*

Often billed as a young reader's book and linked to *Ranald Bannerman's Boyhood* and *Gutta Percha Willie,* this story, which opens in Italy and in which MacDonald describes the major earthquake of 1887 which rocked their home on the Mediterranean coast, is not technically a "children's story." It is *about* the boy Clare Skymer, but is written in a more sophisticated linguistic style than his fairy tales and pure children's fare. *A Rough Shaking*, published in 1890, reprises two of MacDonald's favorite themes, Clare's love for animals (and belief in their immortality), and his quest after fatherhood. MacDonald traces young Clare's life having to fend for himself after the loss of his parents in the earthquake and being taken back to England. His ingenuity in not only

learning to survive on his own, but keeping his goodness intact while trying in some way to help everyone he meets, may be viewed as a fictional portrayal of childhood Christlikeness.

There and Back—*The Cullen Collection Volume 32*

This final installment of the Thomas Wingfold trilogy from 1891 adds yet further dimensions to the personal search for faith and the nature of belief, exemplified in the characters of Barbara Wilder and Richard Tuke. Both Barbara and Richard must ask whether or not God's existence is true, what God's character is like, and what demands are placed upon them as a result. Wingfold's conversations with Barbara probe the foundations of belief with depth and profundity. Wingfold continually emphasizes the great truth: *Everything depends on the kind of God one believes in.* All three of the Wingfold

books address the logic and reasonableness of the Christian faith. MacDonald's characters must *reason out* belief. There will be no pat answers, no "humbug," as he called it. Christianity is reasonable, sensible, intellectually consistent. God's principles are *true.* This *true-ness* pervades MacDonald's worldview as the foundation for Everyman's spiritual quest. As always, the stories upon which MacDonald weaves his spiritual themes are compelling in themselves. *There and Back* is no exception, with mysteries, romance, a disputed inheritance, again with an old castle and library, and a full range of fascinating characters spread along the spectrum of personal development.

The Flight of the Shadow—*The Cullen Collection Volume 33*

MacDonald's second realistic novel written in the first person by a fictional female narrator, almost from its opening pages, *The Flight of the Shadow* feels somber and ominous. It is thus linked with *The Portent* from early in MacDonald's career, both books similar of length and style. Again MacDonald develops his familiar themes through the character of an orphan, who, without an earthly father, must yet discover the goodness of God's Fatherhood. Belorba Whichcote learns of the divine Fatherhood through the goodness of her uncle Edward, who has

raised her on the "old family farm." Both of their lives are complicated when Belorba falls in love with John Day from the neighbouring estate of Rising. John's demonic mother, Lady Cairnedge, who holds a secret over the Whichcote family, threatens to destroy them, foreshadowing the character of Lilith, the first draft of whose saga was being written about the same time as *Flight of the Shadow's* release in 1891. Reconciliation and restoration dispel her evil influence in the end.

Heather and Snow—*The Cullen Collection Volume 34*

This wonderful Scottish tale from 1893, not so expansive of theme and scope as some of MacDonald's lengthier Scottish stories, is yet poignantly moving in its own way. The descriptions of the highlands and the lives of its people are the equal of those in *Castle Warlock* and *What's Mine's Mine*. Who, after reading the story of Kirsty Barclay in *Heather and Snow*, will forget her brother Steenie's cry after "the bonny man!" Indeed, Kirsty is one of MacDonald's most memorable women, whose lifelong friendship with neighbor Francis Gordon is the unifying thread through the story, as both mature from youth into adulthood.

Lilith—*The Cullen Collection Volume 35*

Subtitled, a little oddly, "A Romance," which assuredly it is not, eight distinct manuscript versions of *Lilith* exist, chronicling the book's fitful development under MacDonald's pen until its release in 1895. Some view *Lilith* as the other-worldly climax of MacDonald's literary career. As in *Phantastes*, with which *Lilith* is usually linked, the narrator finds himself embarking on a quest. But unlike the earlier journey into the land of faerie, that of *Lilith* is an inward journey that leads to the world of death, exploring what new self-awarenesses, even repentance, may be possible in that realm. *Lilith* is decidedly dark and difficult to grasp and is not for all readers. MacDonald himself felt that it had been inspired by God as his "final message," though his wife Louisa was troubled by it and counseled her husband not to publish it. This edition for *The Cullen Collection* is unedited in any way.

Salted With Fire—*The Cullen Collection Volume 36*

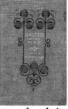

MacDonald's final full length, realistic Scottish novel of 1897, is replete with dense Scottish dialect and spiritual themes. The repentance (through fire) of young minister James Blatherwick, who recognizes the sham of his pretended spirituality, is reminiscent of Thomas Wingfold's spiritual journey. It also embodies in fictional form one of MacDonald's signature themes from his first volume of *Unspoken Sermons*, "The Consuming Fire." Along with these themes, the return of one of MacDonald's favorite character "types," the humble Scottish peasant bard, in the person of cobbler John MacLear, establishes *Salted With Fire* as a work of lasting importance in the MacDonald corpus. It arguably offers a fitting climax to MacDonald's life message. This new edition streamlines the occasionally ponderous Victorian narrative style, and updates the thick Doric dialect into readable English.

Far Above Rubies—*The Cullen Collection Volume 37*

MacDonald's final "novella" of a scant 22,000 words was viewed as so insignificant at the time of its release in 1898 that it never appeared in book form in the U.K and is omitted from many lists of MacDonald's books. Though appearing in magazine form in Britain, its only book edition was published in the United States. For those with eyes to see, however, it reads as an autobiographical retrospective of the beginning of MacDonald's own writing life. Though revealing a poignant final glimpse of MacDonald's waning energy and craft, the significance of its portrait of a struggling youthful author is delightful. Shortly after its writing, what appeared to be a stroke silenced the pen of this remarkable literary genius and man of God. Included in this new edition of *Far Above Rubies* is Ronald MacDonald's memorable portrait of his father from 1910, *From A Northern Window*.

NON-FICTION TITLES ACCOMPANYING
THE CULLEN COLLECTION

*The following synopses (with their somewhat "glowing" descriptions of my work!)
are taken from the Kindle descriptions on Amazon's website.*

George MacDonald A Writer's Life—*Cullen Collection Volume 38*

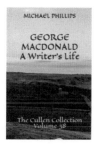

In 1879 George MacDonald said that no biography
should be written of a man still living. He wrote: "I trust
the outer life of one who has written a good many
volumes tending to reveal most that is worth knowing of
his inner life, will be forgotten in this world, after he has
left it...I do not like or approve...of publicizing live
people. If anything is left after a hundred years,
accompanied by a desire to know, then is soon enough."
This major new work thus qualifies as the first biography
of MacDonald written, according to that criteria, more
than a hundred years after his death. It is the longest
biography written about the Scotsman, focusing on the
development and progressive publication of his written works, explaining
how the events of his life contributed to the evolution of that legacy.
Novelist, editor, and publisher of numerous volumes by and about his
mentor, Michael Phillips is recognized as a man with keen insight into
George MacDonald's heart and message. As a best-selling novelist in his
own right, he is doubly qualified to reveal the deeper themes of
MacDonald's writing life. He brings his wisdom to bear on the individual
volumes of *The Cullen Collection of the Fiction of George MacDonald,*
pointing out each book's essential themes, and offering insights into how
each title in MacDonald's fictional corpus can most perceptively be read.
This latest of Phillips' many contributions to MacDonald scholarship, what
he calls a "bibliographic biography," will surely take its place among the
significant illuminations of MacDonald's life and work for many years to
come.

George MacDonald, Scotland's Beloved Storyteller

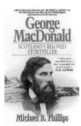

In 1987, Michael Phillips produced the first major biography
of George MacDonald written in the United States. In the
thirty years since that time, his *George MacDonald, Scotland's
Beloved Storyteller* has come to be recognized as a lasting and
significant contribution to the understanding of MacDonald's
life. Phillips' "interpretive portrayal" looks beyond mere
events and probes the essential spiritual themes that informed
the corpus of MacDonald's writings. As time has passed since
its writing, Phillips' own stature as a best-selling devotional
author and novelist has risen alongside his MacDonald work.
Accompanying his own writings, through the years he has continued to
produce numerous new editions of MacDonald's books, as well as studies about
MacDonald. This thirty-year anniversary Kindle edition of *George MacDonald,
Scotland's Beloved Storyteller* is now released in conjunction with *The Cullen
Collection* and Phillips' companion biography of his Scotsman-mentor, *George
MacDonald A Writer's Life.*

Discovering the Character of God
Knowing the Heart of God

Following the enormous response to his updated editions of George MacDonald's novels in the 1980s, Michael Phillips felt the need to introduce MacDonald's fiction readers to the Scotsman's poetry and theological perspectives as well. At the time none of MacDonald's non-fiction writings or poetry was available. Phillips therefore compiled two anthologies of selections, topically arranged, from those writings. Almost thirty years later, the two volumes—*Discovering the Character of God* and *Knowing the Heart of God*—remain classics in the MacDonald

bibliography that have helped multiple thousands probe their understanding of God more deeply. These two clearly organized and understandable illuminations of MacDonald's wisdom distill the essence of MacDonald's thought in manageable topical groupings suitable for devotional reading or more extensive study. Each chapter draws upon selections from the novels and poetry to further inform MacDonald's vision of the infinitely loving and forgiving Fatherhood of God.

George MacDonald's Transformational Theology of the Christian Faith

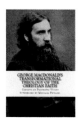

In what he considers one of his most significant contributions to the legacy of George MacDonald, Michael Phillips here presents the complete panorama of George MacDonald's four books of sermons in a single volume. Climaxing a forty-year career making the writings of MacDonald accessible and understandable to the full spectrum of the Christian public— resulting in the publication of over eighty new editions of MacDonald's books—Phillips sets this volume apart from all others, not only as his most ambitious, but perhaps his most important. Presenting twenty of MacDonald's most influential sermons in their full original format, accompanied by his own edited and more understandable copy, Phillips highlights each entry with a concise "Central Thesis," then adds an insightful introduction that illuminates the significant theological ground plowed by MacDonald's pen that, Phillips believes, is destined in time to change how Christendom perceives the underpinings of its faith. What emerges is not only MacDonald's wisdom, but Phillips' own as he shrewdly and perceptively distills what he calls MacDonald's "transformational theology of the Christian faith." Added to the twenty complete sermons are condensed versions of the remaining twenty-nine—each again with a helpful "Central Thesis"—enabling the reader to mine the ore without laboring through dozens of pages of dense and incomprehensibly obscure word-thickets. The result is a massive tome of over 300,000 words comprising all forty-nine of George MacDonald's sermons. It is a volume of incomparable value in understanding the Scotsman's theological foundations.

A Time to Grow

This compilation of brief devotional selections from MacDonald's fiction provides inspirational and thought-provoking daily readings, as well as offering an ideal introduction to the Scotsman's writings. This new edition is perfect for giving friends a taste of MacDonald.

George MacDonald's Spiritual Vision:
An Introductory Overview

Frequently asked through the years, "What did George MacDonald believe?" MacDonald biographer Michael Phillips has prepared this concise overview of MacDonald's perspectives on the essence of true Christian belief. Introducing each of nine points of belief with a knowledgeable summary of MacDonald's position, Phillips draws upon selections from MacDonald's writings to illuminate and succinctly clarify MacDonald's theological orientation on the Godhead, true and false gospels, salvation, the atonement, and other important topics of belief.

TWO TITLES OF SERMON SELECTIONS
Your Life in Christ
The Truth in Jesus

In spite of a gradually expanding awareness of George MacDonald and his influence on the faith and writings of C.S. Lewis, most Lewis devotees, as well as many readers of MacDonald's fantasies and fiction, remain largely unacquainted with the theological foundations of MacDonald's corpus and its influence on Lewis's spiritual development. When intrepid readers attempt to probe MacDonald's sermons, however, most find the going extremely difficult. Expecting Lewis's gift of

straightforward clarity, many readers find MacDonald's Victorian method and syntax daunting and impossible to decipher. Dense theological progressions,

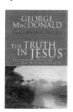

sentences of 100-200 words, and an archaic linguistic style, prevent MacDonald's wisdom from shining through with clarity. In his two volumes *Your Life in Christ* and *The Truth in Jesus,* Michael Phillips addresses this difficulty with the same editorial expertise that distinguish his editions of MacDonald's novels. Assisted by insightful introductions based on his extensive knowledge of MacDonald's writings and thought, these two volumes provide an understandable entrée into the expansive world of George MacDonald's theological writings.

Universal Reconciliation

As an unofficial spokesman for George MacDonald in the minds of thousands who have discovered Phillips's editions of MacDonald's writings since the 1980s, Michael Phillips has been sought out by men and women from around the world to shed light on the complex conundrum presented by the doctrine of eternal punishment. Seeking to address these inquiries in the least controversial way possible, in 1998 Phillips prepared a private compendium of quotes from writers through history, laying out scriptural evidence on both sides of the controversy.

His motive was not to argue for or against any perspective, neither to persuade to a particular point of view, but to give information that would help hungry hearts objectively investigate the matter quietly and personally. Though not made public at the time, Phillips's booklet proved helpful to so many that it is now made more widely available in this new edition. His subtitle aptly summarizes the book's contents: "A selection of quotations by some Christian individuals of repute who have held to the doctrine of universal reconciliation and a list of scriptures upon which their beliefs are based."

George MacDonald and the Late Great Hell Debate

One of the most enduring controversies surrounding the beliefs of George MacDonald for 150 years has been the question: *Was George MacDonald a universalist?* Though his own books contain hints of his theological perspectives on hell, the purpose of God's fire, the atonement, and everlasting punishment, MacDonald stops short of clearly and concisely stating his doctrinal positions unambiguously and without room for misunderstanding. The controversy has therefore raged about what *exactly* MacDonald believed. MacDonald biographer, redactor, and publisher Michael Phillips at last tackles the "great hell debate" head on. With numerous quotes from MacDonald's writings, amplified, interpreted, and understandably explained by his own insights and extensive knowledge of MacDonald's work, Phillips blows the lid off the debate with a clear illumination of the full scope of MacDonald's afterlife vision. This is surely one of the most significant studies of MacDonald's theological perspectives written—a must-read for all serious students of George MacDonald.

ADDITIONAL TITLES OF INTEREST

Accompanying these are the following volumes of my own which some readers through the years have found useful in understanding, interpreting, and exploring the many thematic, literary, and spiritual complexities raised by MacDonald's enormous diversity of writings.

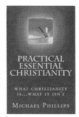
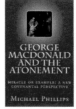

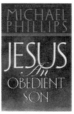

Introductory Selections From

THE CULLEN COLLECTION

Phantastes

1858

The Cullen Collection
Volume 1

— One —

I awoke one morning with the usual perplexity of mind which accompanies the return of consciousness. As I lay and looked through the eastern window of my room, a faint streak of peach- colour, dividing a cloud that just rose above the low swell of the horizon, announced the approach of the sun. As my thoughts, which a deep and apparently dreamless sleep had dissolved, began again to assume crystalline forms, the strange events of the foregoing night presented themselves anew to my wondering consciousness. The day before had been my one-and-twentieth birthday. Among other ceremonies investing me with my legal rights, the keys of an old secretary, in which my father had kept his private papers, had been delivered up to me. As soon as I was left alone, I ordered lights in the chamber where the secretary stood, the first lights that had been there for many a year; for, since my father's death, the room had been left undisturbed. But, as if the darkness had been too long an inmate to be easily expelled, and had dyed with blackness the walls to which, bat-like, it had clung, these tapers served but ill to light up the gloomy hangings, and seemed to throw yet darker shadows into the hollows of the deep-wrought cornice. All the further portions of the room lay shrouded in a mystery whose deepest folds were gathered around the dark oak cabinet which I now approached with a strange mingling of reverence and curiosity. Perhaps, like a geologist, I was about to turn up to the light some of the buried strata of the human world, with its fossil remains charred by passion and petrified by tears. Perhaps I was to learn how my father, whose personal history was unknown to me, had woven his web of story; how he had found the world, and how the world had left him. Perhaps I was to find only the records of lands and moneys, how gotten and how secured; coming down from strange men, and through troublous times, to me, who knew little or nothing of them all.

David Elginbrod
1863

The Cullen Collection
Volume 2

– One –
The Primrose

It was, of course, quite by accident that Hugh Sutherland met Margaret Elginbrod in the fir wood. The wind had changed during the night and swept all the clouds from the face of the sky. And when he looked out in the morning he saw the fir tops waving in the sunlight and heard the sound of a southwest wind sweeping through them with the tune of running waters.

It is a well-practised ear that can tell whether the sound it hears be that of gently falling waters, or of wind flowing through the branches of firs. Sutherland's heart revived at the sound of the genial motions of Nature. He dressed in haste and went out to meet the spring.

Hugh wandered into the heart of the wood. The sunlight shone as a sunset upon the red trunks and boughs of the old fir trees, yet as a sunrise upon the new green fringes that edged the young shoots of the larches. High up hung the memorials of past summers in the rich brown tassels of the clustering cones. The ground under foot was dappled with sunshine on the fallen fir needles, and the great fallen cones which had opened to scatter their autumnal seed now lay waiting for decay. Overhead, the treetops waved in the wind as if to welcome spring.

The wind blew cool, but not cold, and was filled with a delicious odour from the earth, which Sutherland took as a sign that she was coming alive at last. At the foot of a tree he saw a tiny primrose peeping out of its rough leaves...

A little way off, he spied a young girl...leaning against the trunk of a Scotch fir...He went up to her with some shyness.

The Portent

1864

The Cullen Collection
Volume 3

− One −
My Boyhood

My father belonged to the widespread family of the Campbells, and possessed a small landed property in the north of Argyll. But...he was no richer than many a farmer of a few hundred acres...a bare hill formed almost the whole of his possessions. The sheep ate over it, and no doubt found it good. I bounded and climbed all over it, and thought it a kingdom.

From my very childhood, I had rejoiced in being alone. The sense of room about me had been one of my greatest delights. Hence, when my thoughts go back to those old years, it is not the house, nor the family room, nor that in which I slept, that first of all rises before my inward vision, but that desolate hill, the top of which was only a wide expanse of moorland, rugged with height and hollow, and dangerous with deep, dark pools...

There was one spot upon the hill, halfway between the valley and the moorland, which was my favourite haunt...This was my refuge, my home within a home, my study—and, in the hot afternoons, often my sleeping chamber, and my house of dreams...

I had a certain peculiarity of constitution, which I have some reason to believe I inherit. It seems to have its root in an unusual delicacy of hearing, which often conveys to me sounds inaudible to those about me...

Sometimes one awful dread would seize me. That terror was this:—

That the prophetic power manifest in the gift of second sight, which, according to the testimony of my old nurse, had belonged to several of my ancestors, had been in my case transformed in kind without losing its nature, transferring its abode from the *sight* to the *hearing*.

Adela Cathcart

1864

The Cullen Collection
Volume 4

— One —
A Snowy Solitary Ride

The afternoon of Christmas Eve was sinking towards night. All day long the wintry light had been diluted with fog...As I gazed through the window, it was into a vague and mysterious region where anything might be going on, and out of which anything might come without warning. Nothing did come out of it, however, except small sparkles of snow...

Myself and a fellow passenger, of whom I knew nothing, for I had caught but a glimpse of him earlier in the station, sat in a railway carriage, darting along at a frightful rate northwards from London.

Being the sole occupants of the carriage, we had made the most of it, like Englishmen, by taking seats diagonally opposite to each other, laying our heads in the corners and trying to go to sleep...I was going to spend the day, and a few weeks besides, with a very old friend of mine...

How the happy fires were glowing everywhere as we went through the darkened countryside. We shot past many a lighted cottage, and now and then a brilliant mansion. Inside both were hearts like our own, and faces like ours, with the red coming out on them, the red of joy, because it was Christmas. And most of these abodes, large and small, no doubt had some little feast in progress...

I dropped into a sleepy reverie. I was roused from it some time later...We were slowing...We did arrive three minutes later...A servant was waiting for me, and I followed him...to the carriage destined to bear me to "The Swanspond," as my friend Colonel Cathcart's house was called.

Alec Forbes of Howglen

1865

The Cullen Collection
Volume 5

— One —
Burying Day

The farmyard was full of the light of a summer noonday. Not a living creature was to be seen in all the square enclosure, though barns and stables formed the greater part of it, while one end was occupied by a house. Through the gate at the other end, far off in fenced fields, might be seen the dark forms of cattle. And on a road nearer by, a cart crawled along, drawn by one sleepy horse. An occasional weary low came from some imprisoned cow, or animal of the cow-kind, but not even a cat crossed the yard. The door of the empty barn was open and through the opposite doorway shone the last year's ricks of corn, standing golden in the sun.

Although a farmyard is not, either in Scotland or elsewhere, the liveliest of places about noon in the summer, there was a peculiar cause rendering this one, at this moment, exceptionally deserted and dreary. There were, however, a great many more people about the place than usual. But they were all gathered in the nicest room of the house—a room of tolerable size, with a clean boarded floor, a mahogany table black with age, and chairs with high straight backs. Every one of these chairs was occupied by a silent man whose gaze was either fixed on the floor or lost in the voids of space. Most were clothed in black and each wore a black coat. Their hard, thick, brown hands—hands evidently unused to idleness—grasped their knees or, folded in each other, rested upon them.

Annals of a Quiet Neighbourhood

1867

The Cullen Collection
Volume 6

— One —
Walk About a New Town

I am getting old—faster and faster every day. I can help neither the gray hairs nor the wrinkles that gather so slowly yet ruthlessly, nor the quiver I sometimes hear in my voice, nor the sense of being feeble in the knees, even when I only walk across the floor of my study.

I have not got used to age yet. I do not *feel* one atom older than I did at twenty-three. To tell the truth, I feel a good deal younger. For then I only thought that a man had to take up his cross, whereas now I know that a man has to follow Him, and that makes an unspeakable difference.

When my voice quavers, I feel that it is mine and not mine—that it belongs to me like my watch, which does not run so well now, though it ran almost perfectly thirty years ago. And when I feel my knees shake, I think of them with a kind of pity, as I used to think of an old mare of my father's I was very fond of when I was a lad, and which carried me across many a field and over many a fence, but which at last came to have the same weakness in her knees that I now have in mine...

I was thirty when I was made a vicar and first came to this parish, an age at which a man might be expected to be beginning to grow wise. But even then I had much yet to learn.

How vividly I remember the first evening on which I wandered out from the vicarage to take a look about the town of Marshmallows, to see what sort of aspect the sky and earth presented. I had never been here before. The position had been offered me when I was abroad, and I had accepted it without having visited the place.

To be honest, I was depressed. It was depressing weather. Grave doubts as to whether I was in my right place in the church, and whether I was fit to be a pastor, kept rising and floating about, like rain clouds within me. I did not doubt the church, I only doubted myself.

Robert Falconer

1868

The Cullen Collection
Volume 7

– One –
A Recollection

Robert Falconer, schoolboy aged fourteen, thought he had never seen his father. That is, he had no recollection of having ever seen him.

He lived with his grandmother and often retreated to a bare little attic room to be alone with his thoughts. Behind the door, in a recess, stood an empty bedstead, without even a mattress upon it. This was the only piece of furniture in the room, unless some shelves crowded with papers tied up in bundles, and a cupboard in the wall, likewise filled with papers, could be called furniture. There was no carpet on the floor, no windows in the walls. The only light came from the door, and from a small skylight in the sloping roof, which showed that it was a garret-room. Nor did much light come from the open door, for there was no window on the walled stair to which it opened.

Opposite the door a few steps led up into another garret, larger, but with a lower roof, unceiled, and perforated with two or three holes, the panes of glass filling which were no larger than the small blue slates which covered the roof. From these panes a little dim brown light tumbled into the room where the boy now sat on the floor...thinking.

He had recently begun to doubt whether his belief concerning his father was correct. And, as he went on thinking, he became more and more assured that he had seen his father somewhere about six years before, as near as a thoughtful boy of his age could judge of the lapse of a period that would form half of that portion of his existence he could remember at all.

For there dawned upon his memory the vision of one Sunday afternoon...he saw a tall, somewhat haggard-looking man in a shabby black coat, his hat pulled down to his eyebrows, and his shoes very dusty.

Guild Court

1868

The Cullen Collection
Volume 8

— One —
The Walk to the Counting House

In the month of November, not many years ago, a young man was walking from Highbury to the heart of London, known simply as "the City." It was one of those grand mornings that dawn only twice or thrice in the course of the year, and are so independent of times and seasons that November even comes in for its share.

It seemed as if young Thomas Worboise, while readying for the day, had felt the influences of the weather, for he was dressed a trifle more gaily than was altogether suitable for the old age of the year. Neither, however, did he appear in harmony with the bright tone of the morning. A glad west wind was revelling along the streets and up in a lofty blue sky among multitudes of great clouds. There was nothing much for it to do in the woods now, and it took to making merry in the clouds and the streets. And so the whole heaven was full of church windows. Every now and then a great hole in the cloudy mass would shoot a sloped cylinder of sun-rays earthward. Gray billows of vapour with sunny heads tossed about in the air, an ocean for angelic sport. Where the sky shone through it looked awfully sweet and profoundly high.

But though Thomas enjoyed the wind on his right cheek as he passed the streets that opened into High Street, and although certain half sensations, half sentiments awoke in him at its touch, his gaze was cast down at his light trowsers or his enamelled boots, and never rose higher than the shop windows.

The Seaboard Parish

1868

The Cullen Collection
Volume 9

— One —
Homiletic

Dear friends—I am beginning a new book like an old sermon.

As you know, I have been so accustomed to preach all my life, that whatever I say or write will more or less take the shape of a sermon in the end. If you had not by this time learned at least to bear with my oddities, you would not now be reading any more of my teaching.

Indeed, I did not think you would want any more. I thought I had bidden you farewell, But I am seated once again at my writing table, to write for you—with a strange feeling, however, that I am in the heart of some strange and curious acoustic contrivance, by means of which the words which I have a habit of whispering over to myself as I write them, are heard by multitudes of people whom I cannot see or hear. I will favour the fancy that, by a sense of your presence, I may speak more openly and truly, as man to man and author to reader.

Let me suppose for a moment that I am your grandfather, and that you have all come to beg for a story. Let us further suppose that, as usually happens in such cases, I am sitting with a puzzled face, indicating an even more puzzled mind. I know that there are a great many stories in the holes and corners of my brain. But I must find a suitable one. It is a fine thing to be able to give people what they want, if at the same time you can give them what *you* want. To give people only what *they* want, would sometimes be to give them poison. To give them what *you* want, might be to set before them something of which they could not eat a mouthful. What both you and I want, I think, is a dish of good wholesome story-food.

Now I assume the children around me are neither young enough nor old enough to care about a fairy-tale. So that will not do. What they want, I believe, is something that I know about—something that has happened to me.

At the Back of the North Wind

1871

The Cullen Collection
Volume 10

– One –
The Hay Loft

I have been asked to tell you about the back of the north wind. An old Greek writer mentions a people who lived there, and were so comfortable that they could not bear it any longer, and drowned themselves. My story is not the same as his. I do not think Herodotus had got the right account of the place. I am going to tell you how it fared with a boy who went there.

He lived in a low room over a coach-house; and that was not by any means at the back of the north wind, as his mother very well knew. For one side of the room was built only of boards, and the boards were so old that you might run a penknife through into the north wind. And then let them settle between them which was the sharper! I know that when you pulled it out again the wind would be after it like a cat after a mouse, and you would know soon enough you were not at the back of the north wind. Still, this room was not very cold, except when the north wind blew stronger than usual: the room I have to do with now was always cold, except in summer, when the sun took the matter into his own hands. Indeed, I am not sure whether I ought to call it a room at all; for it was just a loft where they kept hay and straw and oats for the horses. And when little Diamond—but stop: I must tell you that his father, who was a coachman, had named him after a favourite horse, and his mother had had no objection:—when little Diamond, then, lay there in bed, he could hear the horses under him munching away in the dark, or moving sleepily in their dreams. For Diamond's father had built him a bed in the loft with boards all round it, because they had so little room in their own end over the coach-house.

Ranald Bannerman's Boyhood

1871

The Cullen Collection
Volume 11

— One —
Introductory

I do not intend to carry my story one month beyond the hour when I saw that my boyhood was gone and my youth arrived—a period determined to some by the first tail-coat, to me by a different sign.

My reason for wishing to tell this first portion of my history is that when I look back, it seems not only so pleasant to me, but so full of meaning, that if I can only tell it right it must prove rather pleasant and not quite unmeaning to those who will read it.

It will prove a very poor story to those who care only for stirring adventures, and like them all the better for a pretty strong infusion of the impossible. But I hope those to whom their own history is interesting—to whom, young as they may be, it is a pleasant thing to be in the world—will find the experience of a boy born in a very different position from most of them, yet as much a boy as any of them, interesting even if somewhat ordinary.

If I did not mention that I, Ranald Bannerman, am a Scotchman, I should be found out before long. For although England and Scotland are in all essentials one, there are such differences between them that one could tell at once, if he had been carried out of the one into the other during the night. I do not mean he might not be puzzled. But unless there had been an intention to puzzle him by a skilful selection of place, the very air, the very colours would tell him where he was. Even if he kept his eyes shut, his ears would tell him without his eyes. But I will not offend fastidious ears with any syllable of my rougher Scot's tongue. I will tell my story in English, and neither part of the country will like it the worse for that.

THE PRINCESS AND THE GOBLIN

1872

The Cullen Collection
Volume 12

– One –
Why the Princess Has a Story About Her

There was once a little princess who—

"But Mr. Author, why do you always write about princesses?"

"Because every little girl is a princess."

"You will make them vain if you tell them that."

"Not if they understand what I mean."

"Then what do you mean?"

"What do you mean by a princess?"

"The daughter of a king."

"Very well, then every little girl is a princess, and there would be no need to say anything about it, except that she is always in danger of forgetting her rank, and behaving as if she had grown out of the mud. I have seen little princesses behave like children of thieves and lying beggars, and that is why they need to be told they are princesses. And that is why when I tell a story of this kind, I like to tell it about a princess. Then I can say better what I mean, because I can then give her every beautiful thing I want her to have."

"Please go on."

There was once a little princess whose father was king over a great country full of mountains and valleys. His palace was built upon one of the mountains, and was very grand and beautiful. The princess, whose name was Irene, was born there, but she was sent soon after her birth, because her mother was not very strong, to be brought up by country people in a large house, half castle, half farmhouse, on the side of another mountain, about half-way between its base and its peak.

The princess was a sweet little creature, and at the time my story begins was about eight years old, I think, but she got older very fast.

Wilfrid Cumbermede

1872

The Cullen Collection
Volume 13

– One –
Introduction

I am—I will not say how old, but well past middle age. This much I feel compelled to mention, because it has long been my opinion that no man should attempt a history of himself until he has set foot upon the border land where the past and the future begin to blend in a consciousness somewhat independent of both, and hence interpreting both. Looking westward, from this vantage-ground, the setting sun is not the less lovely to him that he recalls a merrier time when the shadows fell the other way. Then they sped westward before him, as if to vanish, chased by his advancing footsteps, over the verge of the world. Now they come creeping towards him, lengthening as they come. And they are welcome. Can it be that he would ever have chosen a world without shadows? Was not the trouble of the shadowless noon the dreariest of all? Did he not then long for the curtained queen—the all-shadowy night? And shall he now regard with dismay the setting sun of his earthly life? When he looks back, he sees the farthest cloud of the sun-deserted east alive with a rosy hue. It is the prophecy of the sunset concerning the dawn. For the sun itself is ever a rising sun, and the morning will come though the night should be dark.

In this season of calm weather, when the past has receded so far that he can behold it as in a picture…when he can confess his faults without the bitterness of shame…when his good deeds look poverty-stricken in his eyes, and he would no more claim consideration for them than expect knighthood because he was no thief, when he cares little for his reputation, but much for his character—little for what has gone beyond his control, but endlessly much for what yet remains in his will to determine, then, I think, a man may do well to write his own life.

THE VICAR'S DAUGHTER

1872

The Cullen Collection
Volume 14

– One –
Introductory

My name is Ethelwyn Percivale, and used to be Ethelwyn Walton...I am afraid of writing this, because I am afraid it will be nonsense. But my father tells me that seeing something in print is a great help in recognizing whether it is nonsense or not...

A few days ago my father came home to dinner, and brought with him the publisher of the two books called *The Annals Of a Quiet Neighbourhood* and *The Seaboard Parish*... Mr. S...after some years...had begun again to represent to my father...the necessity for another story to complete the trilogy, as he called it...My father still objected, and... said..."What would you say if I found you a substitute?"...The result of their talk was that my father brought him home to dinner that day, and hence it comes, that, with some real fear and much metaphorical trembling, I am now writing this. I wonder if anybody will ever read it. This my first chapter shall be composed of a little of the talk that passed at our dinner table that day.

"Well, I suppose I had better be as straightforward as I know you would like me to be, Mrs. Percivale. I want you to make up the sum your father owes me. He owed me three books, he has paid me two. I want the third from you."

I laughed, for the very notion of writing a book seemed preposterous.

"I want you, under feigned names of course," he went on, "as are all the names in your father's two books, to give me the further history of the family, and in particular your own experiences in London. I am confident the history of your married life must contain a number of incidents which...might be communicated...to...great advantage."

Gutta Percha Willie

1873

The Cullen Collection
Volume 15

– One –
Who He Was and Where He Was

When he had been at school for about three weeks, the boys called him Six-fingered Jack. But his real name was Willie, for his father and mother gave him the name—not William, but *Willie*, after a brother of his father, who died young, and had always been called Willie.

His name in full was Willie Macmichael. It was generally pronounced Macmickle. A learned anthropologist, for certain reasons which will appear in this history, supposed it to have been the original form of the name, dignified in the course of time into Macmichael.

It was his own father, however, who gave him the name of *Gutta Percha Willie,* the reason of which will also show itself by and by.

Mr. Macmichael was a country doctor who lived in a small village in a thinly-peopled country. He...often had to ride many miles to see a patient, and not unfrequently in the middle of the night. For this hard work he also received very little pay, for a thinly-peopled country is generally a poor country...But the doctor preferred a country life...And he would say to anyone who expressed surprise that, with his reputation, he should remain where he was—"What would become of my little flock if I went away, for there are very few doctors of my experience who would feel inclined to come and undertake my work. I know every man, woman, and child in the whole country-side, and that makes all the difference."...

Willie was a good deal more than nine years of age before he could read a single word...His father had unusual ideas about how he ought to be educated.

Malcolm

1875

The Cullen Collection
Volume 16

— One —
The Corpse

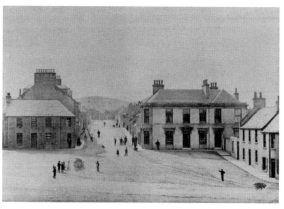

"Na, na. I've got no feelings, I'm thankful to say. I never knew any good to come to them," she said as she entered her parlour. "They just get in the way."

"Nobody ever thought to accuse you of them, mem," said her visitor, Mrs. Mellis, the wife of the town's principal dry-goods dealer who had called ostensibly to console her, but really to see the corpse.

"Indeed, I've always had enough difficulty just to do what I had to do, not to say the thing that nobody would do but myself," went on Miss Horn. "I've had no leisure for feelings and all that."

A brief silence followed.

"Ah, she was taken young," sighed the visitor with long-drawn tones and a shake of the head.

"Not that young," returned Miss Horn. "She was nearly thirty-eight."

"Well, she had a sad time of it, anyway."

"Not that sad, as far as I can see—and who should know better? She had sheltered quarters here, and would have, as long as I was seeing to it. No, it was neither so young nor so sad."

"But she was a patient creature with everyone," persisted Mrs. Mellis, not to be foiled in her attempt to draw out some word of acknowledgment from the former companion of the deceased.

The Wise Woman

1875

The Cullen Collection
Volume 17

– One –

There was a certain country where things used to go rather oddly. For instance, you could never tell whether it was going to rain or hail, or whether or not the milk was going to turn sour. It was impossible to say whether the next baby would be a boy or a girl, or, even after he was a week old, whether he would wake sweet-tempered or cross.

In strict accordance with the peculiar nature of this country of uncertainties, it came to pass one day that, in the midst of a shower of rain that might well be called golden, seeing the sun, shining as it fell, turned all its drops into molten topazes, and every drop was good for a grain of golden corn, or a yellow cowslip, or a buttercup, or a dandelion at least,—while this splendid rain was falling, I say, with a musical patter upon the great leaves of the horse-chestnuts, which hung like Vandyke collars about the necks of the creamy, red-spotted blossoms, and on the leaves of the sycamores, looking as if they had blood in their veins, and on a multitude of flowers, of which some stood up and boldly held out their cups to catch their share, while others cowered down laughing under the soft patting blows of the heavy warm drops;—while this lovely rain was washing all the air clean from the motes, and the bad odours, and the poison seeds that had escaped from their prisons during the long drought—while it fell, splashing, and sparkling, with a hum, and a rush, and a soft clashing—but stop—I am stealing, I find, and not that only, but with clumsy hands spoiling what I steal:—

"O Rain, with your dull two-fold sound,
The clash hard-by, and the murmur all round."

St. George and St. Michael

1876

The Cullen Collection
Volume 18

– One –
Dorothy and Richard

It was the middle of autumn, and had rained all day. Through the lozenge-panes of the wide oriel window the world appeared in the slowly gathering dusk not a little dismal...The room...was large and low, with a dark floor of uncarpeted oak...Although a good fire of logs blazed on the hearth, it was chilly to the old man, who...sat gazing sadly into the flames, which shone rosy through the thin hands spread out before them. At the opposite corner of the great low-arched chimney sat a lady past the prime of life, but still beautiful, though the beauty was all but merged in the loveliness that rises from the heart to the face of such as have taken the greatest step in life—that is, as the old proverb says, the step out of doors. She was plainly yet rather richly dressed, in garments of an old-fashioned and well-preserved look...

They had been talking about the fast-gathering tide of opinion which, driven on by the wind of words, had already begun to beat so furiously against the moles and ramparts of Church and kingdom...

"It is indeed an evil time," said the old man...

In the window sat a girl, gazing from it with the look of a child who could imagine no abatement in the steady downpour.

"We shall leave behind us strong hearts and sound heads," said Mr. Herbert. "And I think there will be none more so than those of your young cousins, my late pupils, of whom I hear brave things from Oxford."

"You will be glad to hear such good news of your relatives, Dorothy," said the lady, addressing her daughter.

Even as she said the words, the setting sun broke through...The girl's hair caught it as she turned her face to answer her mother, and an aureole of brown-tinted gold gleamed for a moment about her head.

Thomas Wingfold Curate

1876

The Cullen Collection
Volume 19

– One –
Helen Lingard

A swift, gray November wind had taken every chimney of the house for an organ pipe, and was roaring in them all at once. Helen Lingard had not been out all day. Having spent the morning writing a long letter to her brother Leopold at Cambridge, she had put off her walk...In the meantime, the wind had risen and brought clouds that threatened rain...

The morning which had given birth to this stormy afternoon had been a fine one, and the curate had gone out for a walk...Yet he had little impulse for activity of any sort. The springs in his well of life did not seem to flow quite fast enough...He knew that he was there and that he answered to *Thomas Wingfold.* But why he was there, and why he was not called something else, he did not know...He had known from the first that he was intended for the church, and had not objected but accepted it as his destiny. But he had taken no great interest in the matter.

The church was to him an ancient institution of approved respectability. He had entered her service. She was his mistress, and in return for the narrow shelter, humble fare, and not quite shabby garments she allotted him, he would perform her observances...

Mrs. Ramshorn had asked the curate to join them...at the dinner hour...

The time came for the curate to take his leave. Bascombe stepped outside with him to have a last cigar...

"Now, I am going to be honest with you," replied Bascombe abruptly, taking the cigar from his mouth. He stopped and turned toward his companion..."Tell me honestly, do you really believe one word of all that?"

The Marquis of Lossie

1877

The Cullen Collection
Volume 20

– One –
The Stable Yard

It was one of those exquisite days that come in every winter, in which it seems no longer the dead body, but the lovely ghost of summer. Such a day bears to its sister of the happier time something of the relation the marble statue bears to the living form. It lifts the soul into a higher region than will summer day of lordliest splendour. It is like the love that loss has purified.

Such, however, were not the thoughts that at the moment occupied the mind of Malcolm Colonsay. Indeed, the loveliness of the morning was but partially visible from the spot where he stood—the stable yard of Lossie House, ancient and roughly paved. It was a hundred years since the stones had been last relaid and levelled. None of the horses of the late Marquis minded it but one—her whom the young man in Highland dress was now grooming—and she would have fidgeted had it been an oak floor. The yard was a long and wide space, with two-storied buildings on all sides of it. In the center of one of them rose the clock, and the morning sun shone red on its tarnished gold. It was an ancient clock, but still capable of keeping good time—good enough, at least, for all the requirements of the house, even when the family was at home, seeing it never stopped, and the church clock was always ordered by it.

It not only set the time, but seemed also to set the fashion of the place, for the whole aspect of it was one of wholesome, weather beaten, time worn existence. One of the good things that accompany good blood is that its possessor does not much mind a shabby coat.

Paul Faber Surgeon

1879

The Cullen Collection
Volume 21

— One —
The Lane

The rector sat on the box of his carriage, driving his horses toward the grand old abbey church of Glaston...

Mr. Bevis drove like a gentleman, in an informal yet thoroughly business-like way...Indeed, the entire effect...gave to the observer that aspect of indifference to show, which, by the suggestion of a nodding acquaintance with poverty, gave it the right clerical air of being not of this world...

The rector was a man about sixty, with keen gray eyes, a good-humoured mouth, and a ruddy face...Altogether he had the look of a man who knew what he was about, and who was on tolerable terms both with himself and his neighbour...Upon the countenance of his wife rested a placidity sinking almost to dullness.

They were passing at good speed through a varying country... Halfway through a very narrow lane, the rector's horses suddenly started and threw up their heads wildly. Sailing high over the hedge bordering the road just in front of them...appeared a great red horse.

Down he came into the road, bearing a tall and certainly handsome rider. A dark brown moustache on a somewhat sunburnt face and a stern settling of the strong yet delicate features gave him a military look.

His blue eyes sparkled as he drew up close to the hedge to make room for the carriage. As he drew near him, Mr. Bevis slackened his speed.

"Hey, Faber," called the clergyman, "you'll break your neck someday...No one in his right senses would make a jump like that."

Sir Gibbie

1879

The Cullen Collection
Volume 22

— One —
The City's Urchin

"Come out o' the gutter, ye nickum!" cried a woman in a harsh, half-masculine voice, standing on the curbstone of a short, narrow, dirty lane at right angles to an important thoroughfare.

About thirty yards from her, a child, apparently about six but in reality about eight, was down on his knees raking with both hands in the grey dirt of the street.

The woman was dressed in dark petticoat and print wrapper. One of her shoes was down at the heel revealing a great hole in her stocking. Had her black hair been brushed, it would have revealed a thready glitter of grey, but all that was now visible of it was only two or three untidy tresses that dropped from under a cap of black net and green ribbons, which looked as if she had slept in it. Her face must have been handsome when it was young but now looked weathered and aging. Her black eyes looked resolute, almost fierce.

At her cry the boy lifted his head, ceased his search, raised himself without getting up and looked at her. They were notable eyes out of which he looked—a deep blue and having long lashes, but more notable for their bewitching expression of confidence. Whatever was at the heart of the expression, it was something that enticed question and might want investigation. The face as well as the eyes was lovely—not very clean but chiefly remarkable from a general effect of something I can only call luminosity. The hair, which stuck out from his head in every direction, would have been of the red-gold kind had it not been sunburned into a sort of human hay. An odd creature altogether the child appeared, as from his bare knees on the curbstone he shook the gutter-drops from his dirty little hands and gazed at the woman of rebuke.

MARY MARSTON

1881

The Cullen Collection
Volume 23

– One –
The Shop

It was an evening early in May. The sun was low, and the street was mottled with the shadows of its cobblestones—smooth enough, but far from evenly set into the ground. The sky was clear, except for a few clouds in the west, hardly visible in the dazzling of the huge setting light. The sun lay among the clouds, just above the horizon, like a radiant liquid that had broken its vessel and was pouring over the fragments. The street was almost empty, and the air was chilly...

The street was not a commonplace one. There were features of interest in the shadowy fronts of almost each of its picturesque old houses...From many a porch and many a latticed oriel window, a long shadow stretched eastward...It was the main street of an old country town, dwindled by the rise of larger and more prosperous places, but holding and exercising a charm none of them would ever gain.

Some of the oldest of its houses, most of them with more than one projecting story, stood about the middle of the street. The central and oldest of these was a draper's shop...

As a place for purchases it might not look promising to some eyes, but both the ladies and the housekeepers of Testbridge knew that rarely could they do better in London itself than at the shop of Turnbull and Marston, whether in variety, quality, or price. And whatever the first impression, the moment the eyes of a stranger began to grow accustomed to its gloom, the size and abundance of the shop looked hopeful indeed...

The shop had a particularly high reputation for all kinds of linen goods, from cambric handkerchiefs to towels, and from table-napkins to sheets.

CASTLE WARLOCK

1881

The Cullen Collection
Volume 24

– One –
Castle Warlock

It was a rough, wild glen to which, far back in times unknown, the family had given its name, and from which it had derived a good deal of its history and its people their character. Glenwarlock lay in the debatable land between Highlands and Lowlands, and most of its inhabitants spoke both Scots and Gaelic. There was often to be found in them a notable mingling of the characteristics of the otherwise widely differing Celt and Teuton. The country produced more barley than wheat, more oats than barley, more heather than oats, more boulders than trees, and more snow than anything.

It was a solitary, thinly peopled region on the eastern edge of the central Scottish Highlands, mostly of bare hills and partially cultivated glens, each with its own small stream, on the banks of which grew here and there a silver birch, a mountain ash, or an alder, but with nothing capable of giving much shade or shelter, except for cliffy banks and big stones. From many a spot you might look in all directions and see no sign of habitation of either man or beast. Even then, however, you might smell the perfume of a peat fire, although you might be long in finding out where it came from. For the houses of that region, if indeed the dwellings could be called houses, were often so hard to distinguish from the ground on which they were built that except for the smoke of peats coming freely out of their wide-mouthed chimneys, it required an experienced eye to discover the human nest.

The valleys that opened northward produced little. There the snow might occasionally be seen lying on patches of still-green oats, destined now only for fodder.

THE PRINCESS AND CURDIE

1882

The Cullen Collection
Volume 25

– One –
The Mountain

Curdie was the son of Peter the miner. He lived with his father and mother in a cottage built on a mountain, and he worked with his father inside the mountain.

A mountain is a strange and awful thing. In old times, without knowing so much of their strangeness and awfulness as we do, people were yet more afraid of mountains. But then somehow they had not come to see how beautiful they are as well as awful, and they hated them—and what people hate they must fear. Now that we have learned to look at them with admiration, perhaps we do not feel quite awe enough of them. To me they are beautiful terrors.

I will try to tell you what they are. They are portions of the heart of the earth that have escaped from the dungeon down below, and rushed up and out. For the heart of the earth is a great wallowing mass, not of blood, as in the hearts of men and animals, but of glowing hot, melted metals and stones. And as our hearts keep us alive, so that great lump of heat keeps the earth alive: it is a huge power of buried sunlight—that is what it is. Now think: out of that cauldron, where all the bubbles would be as big as the Alps if it could get room for its boiling, certain bubbles have bubbled out and escaped—up and away, and there they stand in the cool, cold sky—mountains. Think of the change, and you will no more wonder that there should be something awful about the very look of a mountain: from the darkness—for where the light has nothing to shine upon, much the same as darkness—from the heat, from the endless tumult of boiling unrest—up, with a sudden heavenward shoot, into the wind, and the cold, and the starshine, and a cloak of snow.

Weighed and Wanting

1882

The Cullen Collection
Volume 26

— One —
A Bad Weather Holiday

It was a gray, windy noon at the beginning of autumn. The sky and the sea were almost the same colour. Across from the blurry horizon where they met came troops of waves that broke into white crests as they rushed at the shore. On land the trees and the smoke were greatly troubled—the trees because they would rather stand still, the smoke because it would rather ascend, while the wind kept tossing the former and beating down the latter. None of the hundreds of fishing boats belonging to the coast were to be seen, nor was a single sail visible—not even the smoke of a solitary steamer ploughing through the rain and fog south to London or north to Aberdeen.

To the thousands who had come to Burcliff to enjoy a holiday, the weather was depressing. But whether the labour weary had days or weeks, the holiday had looked short from the beginning, and was growing shorter and shorter, while the dreary days seemed longer and longer.

The Raymounts had come to the east coast of England to enjoy the blue sky, the blue sea, and the bright sun overhead. So far, however, they had scarcely seen any of the three. Their moods were disagreeable.

They found themselves wrapped in a blanket of fog, out of which the water was every now and then squeezed down upon them in the wettest of rains. To those who hated work, this holiday, which by every right and reason belonged to them, seemed snatched away by that vague enemy against whom the grumbling of the world is continually directed. For were they not born to be happy, and how could a human being possibly fulfil that destiny in such miserable circumstances?

Donal Grant

1883

The Cullen Collection
Volume 27

— One —
Foot Faring

It was a lovely morning in the first of summer. Yes, we English, whatever we may end with, always begin with the weather, and not without reason. We have more moods, though are less subject to them, I hope, than the Italians. Therefore we are put in the middle of weather. They have no weather. Where there is so little change, there is at least little to call weather. Weather is the moods of the world, and we need weather good and bad—at one time healing sympathizer with mood, at another fit expression for, at yet another fit corrective to, mood. God only knows in how many ways he causes weather to serve us.

It was a lovely morning in the first of summer. Donal Grant was descending a path on a hillside to the valley below—a sheep track of which he knew every winding better than anyone. But he had never gone down the hill with the feeling that he was not about to go up it again. He was on his way to pastures very new and to him, at this moment, not very inviting. Though his recent past contained the memory of pain, his heart was too full to remain troubled for long—nor was his a heart to harbour care.

A great, billowy waste of mountains lay beyond him, amongst which played the shadows at their games of hide-and-seek. Behind Donal lay a world of dreams into which he dared not turn and look, yet from which he could scarcely avert his eyes.

He was nearing the foot of the hill when he stumbled and almost fell, reminding him of the unpleasant knowledge that the sole of one of his shoes was all but off. Never had he left home for college that his father had not made personal inspection of his shoes to see that they were fit for the journey.

What's Mine's Mine

1886

The Cullen Collection
Volume 28

— One —
The Peregrine Palmer Family

A large fire blazed in the low round-backed grate. A snowy cloth of linen—finer than ordinary, for there was pride in the housekeeping— covered the large, well-appointed table. The silver was bright as the complex motions of butler's elbows could make it, the china ornate though not elegant, the ham large but neither too fat nor too lean. A family of six sat eating breakfast.

Their finery suggested a stark contrast to the rugged landscape surrounding them. What were they doing in such a handsomely furnished dining room in this vast northern wasteland? How did they come to be *there?*

Could they belong—notwithstanding the mirrored oak sideboard, the heavy chairs padded and backed in fawn-coloured morocco leather, and the other accoutrements of what appeared to be a London house inhabited by rich middle-class people, appointed with all the things a dining room "ought" to have, mostly new and entirely expensive—to the clan Ruadh whose very poverty bound the people of this region together? It seemed unlikely.

Beyond the window the western seas lay clear and cold in the distance, broken with islands scattered thinly to the horizon. The ocean looked like a wild yet peaceful mingling of lake and land. Some of the islands were green from shore to shore, others were mere rocks with a bold front to the sea. Over the pale blue sea hung the pale blue sky, flecked with a few cold white clouds high above, looking as if they disowned the earth below. A keen little wind was blowing, crisping the surface of the sea in patches—a pretty large crisping to be seen from the house, for the window looked out over several hills to the sea.

Home Again

1887

The Cullen Collection
Volume 29

— One —
Father and Aunt

In the dusk of the old-fashioned best room of a farmhouse, in the faint glow of the buried sun through the sods of his July grave, two dimly visible elderly persons sat breathing the odour which roses unseen sent through the twilight and open window. One of the two was scarcely conscious of the sweet fragrance, for she did not believe in roses. She believed mainly in mahogany, linen, and hams. To the other it brought too much sadness to be welcomed, for like the sunlight it seemed to come from the grave of his vanished youth.

Richard Colman was not by nature a sad man. He was only one who had found the past more delightful than the present, and had not left his first loves.

The twilight of his years had crept upon him and was steadily deepening, and he felt his youth slowly withering under their fallen leaves. With more education, and perhaps more receptivity than most farmers, he had married a woman he fervently loved…While many of their neighbours were vying with each other in the vain effort to dress, and dwell, and live up to their notion of *gentility*, each in the eyes of the other, Richard Colman and his wife had never troubled themselves about fashion or opinion or what is commonly called "getting ahead," but had each sought to please the taste of the other and cultivate their own…As he sat thus…he was holding closer communion than he knew…with one who seemed to have vanished from all this side of things—except the heart of her husband…

While the elders thus conversed in the dusky drawing room…another couple sat in a little homely foliage-covered shelter in the garden…Richard's son Walter…occupied the wooden bench-seat with his rather distant cousin, Molly Wentworth. For fifteen years the two had been as brother and sister.

THE ELECT LADY

1888

The Cullen Collection
Volume 30

— One —
Landlord's Daughter and Tenant's Son

In a kitchen of moderate size, flagged with slate, unassuming in its appointments, yet clearly looking like more than a mere farmhouse, with the corner of a white pine table between them, sat two young people. They were evidently different in rank and were meeting upon a level other than friendship. The young woman held in her hand the paper which was the subject of their conversation.

She was about twenty-four or twenty-five, well grown and graceful, with dark hair, dark hazel eyes, and somewhat large, handsome features, full of intelligence. It is true there was a look of hardness about her, almost regal—as such features must be until the effects gradually emerge of the prolonged influence of a heart strong in self-subjugation. Her social expression mingled the gentlewoman of education with the landlord's daughter, who was supreme over the household and its share in the labour of production.

As to the young man, it would have required a deeper-seeing eye than falls to the lot of most observers not to take him for a weaker nature than the young woman. Indeed, the deference he showed her as the superior would have added to the difficulty of a true judgment.

He was tall and thin, plainly in fine health. He had a good forehead and clear hazel eyes, not too large or prominent, but full of light. His mouth was firm, and wore a curious smile in the midst of his sunburnt complexion. When perplexed he had a habit of pinching his upper lip between his finger and thumb, which at the present moment he was unconsciously indulging. He was the son of a small farmer—in what part of Scotland is of little consequence.

A Rough Shaking

1890

The Cullen Collection
Volume 31

— One —
How I Came to Know Clare Skymer

It was a day when everything seemed almost perfect. Now and then everything does come nearly right for a moment or two, preparatory to coming all right for good at the last...

I was walking through the thin edge of a little wood of big trees. A slope of green on my left stretched away into the sunny distance...Presently...I heard the tones of a man's voice, both strong and sweet. He was talking to someone in a way I could not understand...

The man looked around, saw me, and turned toward me...I saw before me one nearly, though not quite as old as myself. His hair and beard, both rather long, were quite white. His face was wonderfully handsome, with the stillness of a summer sea upon it. Its features were regular and fine. His white hair and beard gave off a certain radiance from his pale complexion, which I learned afterward, no sun had ever more than browned a little...

The man drew me more and more. He had a way of talking about things seldom mentioned except in dull fashion in the pulpit, as if he cared about them. He spoke of familiar things, but made you feel he was looking out of a high window...This man spoke...in his ordinary voice without an atom of assumed solemnity. They came into his mind as to their home—not as dreams of the night, but as facts of the day...

In short, I was drawn to the man as never to another...I saw at once that I was greatly Skymer's inferior...I soon ceased to think of him as my new friend, for I seemed to have known him before I was born...I am going to tell the early part of his history. If only I could tell it as it deserves to be told...I shall tell the story as...a narrative of my *own* concerning him.

THERE AND BACK

1891

The Cullen Collection
Volume 32

– One –
Bookbinder and Son

 Stretching his aching muscles and straightening from his book, John Tuke rested his glance on his son Richard. A fine strong lad, Tuke thought as he observed the boy at work. And such skilled hands! Hands I never thought could produce such skill in the trade.

But clumsiness or ugliness in infancy is sometimes promise of grace or beauty in manhood. In Richard's case, the promise was fulfilled—what had seemed repulsive to some who beheld him as an infant had given place to a certain winsomeness. He was now a handsome, well-grown youth, with dark brown hair, dark green eyes, broad shoulders, and a bit of a stoop which made his mother uneasy. But he had good health, and what was better, an even temper, and what was better still, a willing heart toward his neighbour. A certain overhanging of his brow was called a scowl by those who did not love him, but it was of minor significance—probably the trick of some ancestor.

With pride—not the possessiveness of the owner, but the liberating joy of the mentor—John Tuke watched in silence as the skilful fingers of the seventeen-year-old youth moved lovingly over the volume under his care. Richard occasionally assisted his father in binding, but in general, as now, he occupied himself with his own particular devotion—the restoration of antiquity.

While learning the bookbinding trade, Richard had attended evening classes at King's College, where he developed a true love for the best of literature, especially from the sixteenth century. He grew to possess a peculiar regard for old books, and with the three or four shillings a week at his disposal, searched about to discover and buy volumes that, for their physical condition, would be of little worth to the bookseller. With these for his first "patients," he opened a hospital for the lodging, restorative treatment, and invigoration of decayed volumes.

The Flight of the Shadow

1891

The Cullen Collection
Volume 33

– One –
A Look Back

I am old. Otherwise I do not think I would have the courage to tell the story I am going to tell.

All those concerned in it about whose feelings I am careful, are gone where, thank God, there are no secrets! If they know what I am doing, I know they do not mind. If they were alive to read what I record, they might perhaps now and again look a little paler and wish the page turned. But to see the things set down would not make them unhappy: they do not love secrecy.

Half the misery in the world comes from trying to *look*, instead of trying to *be*, what one is not. I would that not God only but all good men and women might see me through and through. They would not be pleased with everything they saw, but then neither am I. And I would have no coals of fire in my soul's pockets!

But my very nature would shudder at the thought of letting one person that loved a secret see into it. Such a one never sees things as they are. They would not see what was there, but something shaped and coloured after their own likeness. No one who loves and chooses a secret can be of the pure in heart that shall see God.

Yet how shall I tell even who I am?

Which of us is other than a secret to all but God! Which of us can touch the mystery of life—that One who is not myself has made me able to say *I*—and thus tell, with poorest approximation, what he or she is! How little can any of us tell about even those ancestors whose names we know.

HEATHER AND SNOW

1893

The Cullen Collection
Volume 34

– One –
The Race

Upon neighbouring stones, held fast to the earth like two islands of an archipelago in an ocean of heather, sat a boy and a girl. The girl was knitting, or, as she would have called it, *weaving* a stocking. With his eyes fixed on her face, the boy was talking excitedly in an animated voice. He had great fluency, and could have talked just as fast in good English as in the dialect in which he was now pouring out his ambitions—the broad Saxon of Aberdeen. They were both about fifteen.

The boy was telling the girl that he meant to be a soldier like his father, and quite as good a one too. He knew so little of himself or the world, and was so moved by the results he anticipated without regard for the actions it would take on his part to reach them, that he saw success as already his, with a grateful country at his feet. His inspiration was so purely self-motivated ambition that even if he were to achieve much for his country, Kirsty doubted that she would owe him much gratitude.

"I'll not have the world make light of *me!*" he said.

"Maybe the world winna trouble itself about ye so muckle as to think of ye at all!" returned his companion quietly.

"Why are ye scoffin' at me?" retorted the boy, rising and looking down on her in displeasure. "A body canna let his thoughts go but ye're doon upon them like birds upon corn!"

"I wouldna be scoffin' at ye, Francie, but that I care too muckle about ye to let ye think I hold the same opinion of ye that ye have of yerself," answered the girl, who went on with her knitting as she spoke.

Lilith

1895

The Cullen Collection
Volume 35

− One −
The Library

I had just finished my studies at Oxford, and was taking a brief holiday from work before assuming definitely the management of the estate. My father died when I was yet a child; my mother followed him within a year; and I was nearly as much alone in the world as a man might find himself.

I had made little acquaintance with the history of my ancestors. Almost the only thing I knew concerning them was, that a notable number of them had been given to study. I had myself so far inherited the tendency as to devote a good deal of my time, though, I confess, after a somewhat desultory fashion, to the physical sciences. It was chiefly the wonder they woke that drew me. I was constantly seeing, and on the outlook to see, strange analogies, not only between the facts of different sciences of the same order, or between physical and metaphysical facts, but between physical hypotheses and suggestions glimmering out of the metaphysical dreams into which I was in the habit of falling. I was at the same time much given to a premature indulgence of the impulse to turn hypothesis into theory. Of my mental peculiarities there is no occasion to say more.

The house as well as the family was of some antiquity, but no description of it is necessary to the understanding of my narrative. It contained a fine library, whose growth began before the invention of printing, and had continued to my own time, greatly influenced, of course, by changes of taste and pursuit. Nothing surely can more impress upon a man the transitory nature of possession than his succeeding to an ancient property! Like a moving panorama mine has passed from before many eyes, and is now slowly flitting from before my own.

Salted With Fire

1897

The Cullen Collection
Volume 36

— One —
The Cobbler

"Whaur are ye off to this bonny mornin', Maggie, my doo?" said the cobbler, looking toward his daughter as she stood in the doorway with her own shoes in her hand.

"Jist over to Stonecross, wi' yer permission, father, to ask the mistress for a few handfuls of chaff. Yer bed's grown a mite hungry for more."

"Hoot, the bed's weel enough, lassie!"

"It's anything but weel enough. 'Tis my part to look after my ain father, an' see that there be no knots in either his bed or his porridge."

"Ye're jist like yer mither all over again, lass! Weel, I winna miss ye that much, for the minister Pethrie'll be in this mornin'."

"Hoo do ye ken that, father?"

"We didna agree very weel last night, an' I'm thinkin' he'll be back, nae jist for his shoes, but to finish his argument."

"I canna bide that man—he's such a quarrelsome body!"

"Toots, bairn! I dinna like to hear ye speak scornful of the good man that has the care of oor souls."

"It would be more to the purpose if ye had the care of his!"

"An' so I have. Hasna everybody the care of every other's?"

"Ay. But he presumes upon it—an' ye dinna. That's the difference!"

Far Above Rubies

1898

The Cullen Collection
Volume 37

– One –
Hector Macintosh

Hector Macintosh was a young man about twenty-five, who, with the proclivities of the Celt, inherited also some of the consequent disabilities, as well as some that were accidental.

Among the rest was a strong tendency to regard only the ideal...His chief delight lay in the attempt to embody, in...the natural form of verse, the thoughts that were constantly moving in him toward that ideal, even when he was most conscious of his inability to attain to their poetic utterance.

It was only in the solitude of his own chamber that he attempted their embodiment. Of all things, he shrank from any discussion of his most cherished matters of mind and heart. Nor, indeed, had he any friends with whom he was tempted to share his deepest and best thoughts. In truth, he was intimate with none.

His mind dwelt much upon love and friendship in the imaginary abstract, but of neither did he have the smallest immediate experience. He held to the highest and purest ideals, and seemed to find satisfaction enough in the endeavour to embody them in his poetry, without desiring or even imagining communicating them publicly.

The era had not yet dawned when every scribbler is consumed with the vain ambition of being recognized, not, indeed, as what he is, but as what he pictures himself in his secret sessions of thought. That disease could hardly attack him while yet his very imagination recoiled at the thought of such a hostile presence invading his consciousness. Whether this was modesty, or had its hidden base in conceit, I am, with the few insights I have into his mind, unable to determine.

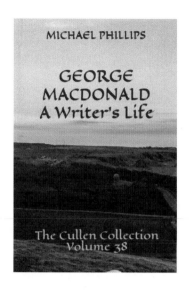

MICHAEL PHILLIPS

GEORGE
MACDONALD
A Writer's Life

The Cullen Collection
Volume 38

George
MacDonald
Λ WRITER'S LIFE

2018

The Cullen Collection
Volume 38

Introduction

George MacDonald A Writer's Life offers a *perspective* of George MacDonald's life (1824-1905) viewed through the lens of the written legacy of works he has left to posterity. Our focus is those writings themselves, with special emphasis on his realistic and fantasy novels, and their sequence of writing as they emerged out of the events and circumstances of MacDonald's life.

This focus on MacDonald's fiction is not intended to overlook the significance and value of the other varied genres of MacDonald's expansive corpus. It simply happens to be the emphasis of *this* particular work as giving a somewhat unique vantage point from which to assess MacDonald's life, and from which to most insightfully read his fiction. His sermons, essays, poetry, and short stories wonderfully illuminate MacDonald's legacy as well.

My work through the years has focused primarily on MacDonald's novels and sermons, because that is where I have felt I could do the most good, with revised and updated editions that make MacDonald's stories and spiritual ideas more accessible to contemporary readers. I have produced six volumes that do that for the sermons. The books of this series will hopefully accomplish that purpose for MacDonald's fiction, in addition to making them more widely available.

Eighteen of the volumes in *The Cullen Collection* are updated and expanded titles from the Bethany House series of edited MacDonald novels published in the 1980s. Limitations of length dictated much about how those previous volumes were produced. To interest a publisher in the project during those years when MacDonald was a virtual unknown, certain sacrifices had to be made. Cuts to length had to be more severe than I would have preferred. Practicality drove the effort. Imperfect as those editions were in some respects, they helped inaugurate a worldwide renaissance of interest in MacDonald. They were wonderful door-openers for many thousands into MacDonald's world.

Hopefully this new and more comprehensive set of MacDonald's fiction will take up where they left off. Not constrained by the limitations that dictated production of the former volumes, these new editions reflect MacDonald's originals more closely, while still preserving the flavor, pace, and readability of their predecessors. Nineteen additional titles have been added. The thirteen realistic novels among these have been updated according to the same priorities that guided the earlier Bethany House series. That process will be explained in more detail in the introductions to the books of the series. The final six, which would more accurately be termed "fantasy," have not been edited in any way. They are faithful reproductions of the originals exactly as they were first published. These six—*Phantastes, At the Back of the North Wind, The Princess and the Goblin, The Wise Woman, The Princess and Curdie,* and *Lilith*—

are so well known and have been published in so many editions through the years, that it has seemed best to reproduce them in this series with the same texts by which they are generally known.

The books of this series are "redacted" editions. *Redaction* is a little-understood term that in our time has come to carry unfortunate implications in the political realm almost synonymous with censorship. When portions of a document are blacked out, it is said to have been "redacted." That is actually an incorrect use of the word. Redaction involves the preparation and readying of texts for *publication*—not simply the elimination of material you don't want someone else to see. This may involve editing, revising, or condensing, but it is not primarily a function of length. It means preparing texts (revising and updating as needed) for a newly published edition.

Therefore, I use the term redaction to describe the many varying facets of my work in preparing new editions of MacDonald's writings for publications. Editing, revising, and updating may be called for, sometimes more, sometimes less. For other titles an introduction and new format is all that is involved.

Several comprehensive biographies of George MacDonald exist, and numerous smaller ones. The standard work on George MacDonald's life was published in 1924 by his son Greville, entitled *George MacDonald and His Wife.* No other major biography was written for over sixty years, until 1987 when two new biographies appeared independently—William Raeper's *George MacDonald*, published in the U.K., and my own *George MacDonald Scotland's Beloved Storyteller* in the U.S. MacDonald pioneer and scholar, Wheaton College professor Dr. Rolland Hein, added another significant work to this list in 1993 with his *George MacDonald, Victorian Mythmaker.* It was followed the next year, 1994, by Dr. Glenn Edward Sadler's biographically organized collection entitled, *An Expression of Character: The Letters of George MacDonald.* Many other biographical sources exist, and no doubt many will continue to be added as MacDonald studies continue, but these are the major works at the present time.

This new "bibliographic biography" is comprised of the introductions to the thirty-seven volumes of *The Cullen Collection,* presented in the sequence of their original writing. These introductions have a twofold purpose—to give a continuous and sequential perspective of George MacDonald's life leading up to the writing of the individual books, and to acquaint readers with the background, themes, and uniqueness of each book and its publication. Both these purposes will hopefully allow MacDonald's writings to be read with greater insight. Using his life's circumstances to illuminate his work and stringing these introductions together in this final volume of the series, gives an overview of MacDonald's corpus of fiction works as it grew out of the events of his life. The fiction works, not minutiae of events, remain the focus.

This "life story" has a very specific purpose as it moves through MacDonald's life—that is to shine light on MacDonald's written works, with special attention focused on his fiction, and to highlight MacDonald's legacy as one of the Victorian era's prolific and significant novelists. In what way this somewhat unusual biography may be categorized in a technical sense is unimportant if it serves the objective of illuminating MacDonald's life and helps us appreciate his written legacy with deeper understanding.

In writing the thirty-seven introductions for *The Cullen Collection,* my purpose has been for readers to encounter the unfolding of George MacDonald's forty-year professional "writer's life" in conjunction with a progressive reading of his corpus of fiction. Those years and these introductions span the forty-year period from 1858 to 1898, from the year the first book of this set was published to the year of MacDonald's final published work. I hope that presenting them in this single volume will also have value for those desiring to read of that life as a continuous whole, perhaps before they turn to the works themselves.

These two objectives are not necessarily in perfect harmony at every point. Trying to achieve both these distinct purposes—*introduce the individual novels* in the progression of their writing and publication, and at the same time *tell a continuous life story* in a single volume—has necessarily resulted in overlap and redundancies.

Occasional extensive quotes from the novels have value in this "writer's life" as giving the flavor of certain books. These selections, however, will be redundant for one who is about to read the novel itself and who will soon encounter the same passage again. In the same way, certain discussions about MacDonald's use of dialect, for instance, or my own editorial work, or the historical progression of MacDonald studies and publications, may be repeated in different contexts for some of the novels for the benefit of those who may read only that particular book. This again will create inevitable redundancy for those reading this writer's life as a single continuous story.

Such overlap cannot be helped given that I am attempting to accomplish two objectives at once—with some material more appropriate for the individual volumes, and other material more appropriate for this overview. I assume readers will be able to intelligently and objectively navigate the anomalies and idiosyncrasies of this unique and ambitious project in conjunction with their own particular reading program.

Additionally, I am aware that there will be diverse classes of people reading these introductions. Some come to MacDonald primarily for his stories. Others may come to this writer's life with a keen interest in biographical facts. The first group may find the extensive footnotes distracting and uninteresting, wondering why I am drifting so far into the weeds of detail. Others may be entirely fascinated by the discussion of first editions, or which noted authoress was instrumental in the publication of *David Elginbrod*, or whether there was in fact a "great library in the north" in MacDonald's youth, or in the distinctions between the versions of *Robert Falconer*, or in the impact of U.S. library editions on MacDonald's income, or whether or not C.S. Lewis's perspective of MacDonald as a second-rate novelist holds water, or which is the true first edition of *Castle Warlock* or *Salted With Fire*. If you are uninterested in my investigations into such matters, by all means skip the footnotes. If you find such questions fascinating, perhaps you may be one who will be able to provide *more* information about one or another of the various conundrums that have eluded MacDonald biographers for 100 years!

Again, everyone will read according to their own interests. I realize that I am trying to be "all things to all men," even though I am well aware that no author can please all the people all the time.

As will be clear as we go along, MacDonald's books were published in both the U.K. and the U.S., usually (but not always) with the distinctive British spellings (neighbourhood, colour, favourite, labour, etc.) changed in the American editions (to neighborhood, color, favorite, labor). For the novels themselves, and quotes referenced from them, I have preserved most British spellings because that is how MacDonald originally wrote them. (Even these spellings, however, are not always consistent in MacDonald's originals.) In my introductions, when I am speaking for *myself,* I use the American spellings because I am an American and that is how *I* write. In quoting from other books and authors, some British and some American, I obviously retain the usage of the original source.

This new work emerges out of perspectives presented occasionally in more detail in my own prior work, *George MacDonald Scotland's Beloved Storyteller,* as well as certain other of my writings. I felt that it would be distracting and redundant to attempt referencing and footnoting every parallel in those books. I *have* quoted freely and at length, however, from two of my fellow biographers, Rolland Hein and William Raeper, where they offer perspective that sheds light on some aspect of MacDonald's life that I find especially valuable, and where they provide insight beyond my own. Citations from their books are, of course, fully footnoted.

None of us who study MacDonald are able to give a complete picture of his life and work. We are all peering back in time through our individual prisms of perspective. Though we are historians and biographers trying to give breadth and depth to the significance of MacDonald's life, mostly we are *interpreters* of his life. The perspectives we offer combine and enhance each other. Hopefully, all taken together, they indeed offer a reasonably rounded portrayal of a remarkable man and his huge and diverse life's work. I am greatly indebted to and appreciative of both Hein's and Raeper's insights and extensive research, along with Glenn Sadler's, and share them along with my own to provide readers a broad panorama of viewpoints, as we all contribute in our own way to breathing new life into this man's legacy.

More on the backgrounds of these new editions, why the series is called *The Cullen Collection,* and specifics regarding my continuing work in reissuing, redacting, and republishing George MacDonald's writings, will be detailed in the individual volumes of the series.

Michael Phillips
Cullen, Morayshire
Scotland, 2018

www.TheCullenCollection.com

www.FatherOfTheInklings.com

www.WisePathBooks.com